# OPERATION WEREWOLF

During the closing months of the war Nazi
Germany hurled a terrifying new force
against the advancing Allies: the Werewolves.
Blood-mad fanatics, they stopped at nothing
in their savage defence of the dying Reich.
Their leader, and the most ruthless of all,
was the Hawk, *Obersturmbannführer* Horst
Habicht, commander of the legendary
Alpine Redoubt. The Destroyers, the hand-
picked killers led by Lieutenant Crooke, VC,
were given their deadliest mission yet: to
penetrate the Hawk's mountain fortress and
kill him. The only way in was through the
ranks of the Werewolves...

# OPERATION WEREWOLF

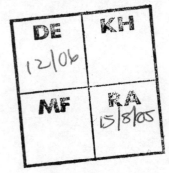

# OPERATION WEREWOLF

*by*

Charles Whiting

**Magna Large Print Books**
Long Preston, North Yorkshire,
BD23 4ND, England.

British Library Cataloguing in Publication Data.

Whiting, Charles
   Operation werewolf.

   A catalogue record of this book is
   available from the British Library

   ISBN   0-7505-2378-6

First published in Great Britain in 1976 by Seeley Service & Co.

Copyright © Charles Whiting 1976

Cover illustration © André Leonard by arrangement with
P.W.A. International Ltd.

The moral right of the author has been asserted

Published in Large Print 2005 by arrangement with
Eskdale Publishing Ltd.

Magna Large Print is an imprint of Library Magna Books Ltd.

Printed and bound in Great Britain by
T.J. (International) Ltd., Cornwall, PL28 8RW

'Operation Werewolf must destroy these Nazi fanatics before they get established – or God help this country!'

*Commander Mallory, Naval Intelligence,*

*April 1945*

## Section One

## THE LAST MISSION

'The Werewolf is the start of a massive German resistance movement which some of our top intelligence people think might prolong the war another twelve months more if we don't crush it now.'

*Commander Mallory, Naval Intelligence,*
*to Lt Crooke, CO of the Destroyers,*
*April 1945*

# ONE

Major John Poston pushed back his dark brown XI Hussars beret with the red band and wiped the sweat from his face. Screwing up his eyes against the glare of the spring sunshine he stared at the bullet-pocked yellow sign post and read the distances on it out loud, 'Ülzen eleven kilometres, Hanstedt thirteen.'

He took in the scene at the crossroads – the burnt-out Sherman and beside it a cluster of helmet-hung wooden crosses, the white verge-tapes indicating the area that had been cleared of mines, the shell holes in the fields.

Obviously British troops had been this way but had the cobbled road running off to the left been cleared of enemy stragglers? Major Poston knew that the 'Master', as

Montgomery's youthful liaison officers called their chief, did not like them to take the side roads. They were too dangerous for the lone jeep rider. But the road was obviously a short cut back to the Field-Marshal's HQ.

He loosened his .38 and put the jeep into gear. He'd chance it. Swinging the wheel round, he turned off the main road.

It was a beautiful afternoon, Lüneburg Heath was bright with wild flowers and the air was heavy with the smell of pines. Poston, who had been one of the Master's 'eyes and ears' since they had met in the desert nearly three years earlier, drove slowly, enjoying this brief time out of war, but from the far distance came a reminder that nearly a million men were still locked in deadly combat – the steady rumble of the heavy guns, permanent background music to the war.

Poston had just negotiated a tree left across the road by the retreating *Wehrmacht* and was picking up speed again when a little blonde girl in white socks darted into the road. He hit the brakes hard. The jeep skidded to a stop only feet from her.

'*Was ist los?*' he called.

The little girl did not reply. Her hands were folded behind her back, as children do when they are about to ask a favour of an adult.

'*Willst du Schokolade?*' Poston asked.

'*Nix Schokolade,*' the little girl said. Suddenly she brought her right hand round to the front.

'*You little bitch!*' The words died on Poston's lips as he saw the stick grenade she was holding. He flung himself out of the jeep; she threw it and sprang back. The potato masher exploded under the right wheel of the jeep and an agonizing pain shot through Poston's right leg. But he had no time to worry about the wound. As he dragged himself towards the cover of the ditch he realized that he had driven right into a neatly planned ambush. He would have to fight for his life. For although the skinny youths in the black uniform of the

Hitler Youth who were now running from the pine forest on both sides of the road could not have been more than fourteen, the Schmeisser machine pistols they were carrying looked purposeful enough. Lead ripped up the road all about him. Slugs whined over his head. He screamed as one hit him in the ribs. Pulling out his revolver he fired a couple of wild shots at the boys.

One of them dropped suddenly and the others hesitated.

Poston seized the opportunity and began to crawl towards the ditch again, blood streaming from his two wounds. Once there he knew he had a chance of survival. But suddenly a freckle-faced boy loomed up in front of him. Poston saw the big fowling piece he carried and tried to raise his revolver, but the boy was quicker. A skinny leg shot out and kicked the .38 from his hand. Poston stared up at him numbly, as he raised the heavy gun. The boy seemed to take ages before he got it into the firing position. He pointed the double barrel straight at the dying Major's face and squeezed the trigger. The impact at such short range lifted Poston from the road. He was dead before he hit the cobbles again.

The black-clad boys stared down at the dead officer in stunned silence. Behind them the little blonde girl sat in the wrecked jeep. In one hand she held a shabby rag doll.

'Is he really dead?' one of the boys asked.

The tallest of the group nodded. 'Yes, he's dead all right. He looks like my grandfather when the lightning struck him during the haymaking.'

In the distance the rumble of the guns was drowned now by the rusty rattle of tank tracks. *'Panzer – Tommies!'* the boy with the fowling piece called from further up the road where he stood guard. 'Two of them!'

The boys looked at the one they called Horst. 'Are you going to do it?' one of them asked.

Horst hesitated. 'I don't know,' he said slowly. 'Why always me?'

The noise of the tanks was getting closer. By the tree that blocked the road the boy with the fowling piece shouted over his shoulder. 'They're two hundred metres away! Two Churchills!'

Horst picked up a stick and dipped it in the pool of blood in which the Major lay.

'Go on,' the other boys urged.

Horst let the stick drop. 'I can't,' he said.

'Let me do it, Horst. *Bitte-bitte!*'

It was the little girl. She jumped down from the jeep and, still clutching her rag doll, picked up the stick and dipped it in the officer's blood again.

The tanks were getting very close now but their nearness did not worry the little girl. With her head cocked on one side, she drew the single letter in a large childish hand. Then, as the first tank began to push aside the tree, she threw the stick away. For one moment she stared at her work in silence. Then she turned to the others. *'Los,'* she cried. *'Hauen wir ab!'*

They turned and began to run. Seconds later they had vanished into the pine wood as the first tank came to a stop and the troop commander, a sergeant, poked his head cautiously over the top of the turret. He checked the ditches on both sides of the road. Satisfied that no young fanatic was lurking there, he clambered out of the turret, sten gun in hand, and walked over to the dead officer. Behind him followed the gunner. Together they stared down at the dead Major in silence.

'Owt we can do, Sarge?' the gunner asked.

The NCO shook his head. 'Not a sausage, Curly. The poor sod's a gonner all right.'

The gunner nodded. 'Ay, tha's right there, Sarge. And what a bloody rotten time to buy it!' The two men stared down at the officer. Then the gunner tapped the sergeant on the arm. 'What do you make o' that, Sarge?' he asked.

'Make of what?'

'That mark on the road! Happen it was writ with his own blood. It looks like a W.'

The two soldiers stared down at the strange red mark, which was already beginning to fade in the hot sun.

# TWO

Commander Mallory, the assistant to the head of Naval Intelligence, leaned against the mantelpiece of Room 39, which housed the Admiralty's own Secret Service, and ran his eye over the 'Most Immediate' once more. Soon he would be leaving the Senior Service, after six years in Naval Intelligence, but the message had come from the Prime Minister and Mr Churchill expected prompt action even from those temporary officers whose minds were now full of demobilization and plans for the future.

He stubbed out his three-ringed Morland Special, which he had made for him in a shop in Bond Street, and pressed the brass bell on the desk.

A Wren poked her nose round the door. 'Yes, Commander?'

'Could you get me Lieutenant Crooke, please?'

'Yes, sir,' she said, and vanished.

Mallory walked towards the high windows and gazed out at the Horse Guards Parade. He could just make out the private entrance to No 10 Downing Street. He noted that the barrage balloon which usually hovered over the place had gone. Its absence seemed yet another sign that the war was almost over. But he knew that the Prime Minister's worries on the score were not altogether gone. The 'Most Immediate' which he held in his hand and the flood of alarming messages from SHAEF Intelligence in Rheims this last week showed that clearly enough. With their capital surrounded and most of their territory occupied by the victorious troops of the Allied armies in both west and east, it seemed that the Germans were finished. Yet...

There was a polite knock on the door. A moment later a tall thin officer in khaki entered, the purple ribbon of the Victoria

Cross decorating his breast. It had also cost him an eye, the empty socket of which was covered with a black patch.

Mallory looked up in surprise. 'What's this, Crooke? Back in khaki?'

Crooke nodded and pointed to the badge on his beret. 'Yes. I've been accepted for the Special Air Service. They're flying me out to the Far East next week.' He took off the beret and sat down. 'The war's virtually over in Europe now. You don't need me and the Destroyers any more.' He referred to the special commando squad run by Naval Intelligence. 'After all I am a regular soldier and I've been swanning around with the Destroyers for nearly three years now. I've got to start thinking of my career again – or what's left of it!'

Mallory knew what he meant. After Crooke had lost his eye in 1942, the authorities had refused to allow him to return to the front. In his determination not to be tied to a chairborne job in the War Office, he had struck the Deputy Commander, Home

Forces on the nose. He had been demoted from colonel to second lieutenant and only his Victoria Cross had saved him from a full-scale court martial. But Alan Brooke, the Chief of the Imperial General Staff, had sworn that Crooke would never be promoted again as long as he ran the British Army. With Mallory's help he had escaped the Field-Marshal's wrath and taken over the command of Naval Intelligence's Destroyers, recruited from Cairo's military prison. With the full backing of the Director of Naval Intelligence, the Destroyers had carried out special undercover missions all over Europe during the last three years. But now that the war was nearly over there would, as Crooke realized, but no further need for their services.

Mallory lit another cigarette. 'I don't think you should be too hasty about the De-stroyers' future,' he said. 'I know everybody's thinking about demob these days, but before you make any final decision about the SAS posting take a look at this.' He passed the

Prime Minister's 'Most Immediate' over the desk to Crooke.

The Destroyers' boss read through it quickly.

'Well?'

'Montgomery's very cut up about Poston's death. Apparently he had been with the Field-Marshal for nearly three years. Really one of his blue-eyed boys. He went right to the top, to the PM himself, to get permission to use your bunch of rogues on the job.'

'Good of the military establishment to recognize the fact that the Destroyers still have some use, now that the war's virtually over. What's so important about the death of one of the Field-Marshal's liaison staff? There are plenty more young men eager to be close to the source of power, I'm sure.'

'Naturally. It just happens that Poston was the most important of the thirty odd British and American soldiers killed under similar circumstances in the Second and Twelfth Army Groups in the last week or so. And in each case something like this was found on their bodies.' He reached into the pocket of his uniform and brought out a simple card decorated with a crude skull-and-crossbones and the letter 'W'. Its one edge was stained red. Crooke picked up the card and stared at it.

'What does the "W" stand for?'

'*Werwolf.*' Mallory pronounced the German word perfectly. He had spent a year in the German-speaking part of Switzerland after leaving Eton and had an excellent command of the language. 'Harmless-looking civvies, men and women and children – especially children – transformed suddenly into bloodthirsty killers, picking off lone Allied soldiers, stupid or unfortunate enough to stray off the main lines of communication. The Werewolf is the start of a massive German resistance movement which some of our top intelligence people think might prolong the war another twelve months, if we don't crush it now. Do you understand – another twelve months!'

Crooke nodded.

'This country can't afford another year of total war. The barrel is about scraped clean. Two months ago the government called up the forty-five-year-olds. We're virtually broke. A third of our Empire is in Jap hands. The nation simply couldn't stand another year of the war in Europe. Regardless of whether it was full-scale or guerrilla war the man in the street in this country would crack up. He wouldn't be able to bear the strain. And we know what that would mean for us politically, don't we?'

'A socialist take-over?'

'Yes, Attlee's lot of parlour pinks are powerful enough as it is. If the PM can't give the country a final victory over Germany this summer, the next election will be a Labour walkover. This will be the Destroyers' *last* mission. Operation Werewolf *must* destroy these Nazi fanatics before they get established – or God help this country!'

# THREE

'Funnily enough the Boche made no attempt to start up a resistance movement the moment we crossed the German frontier last September,' Mallory said. 'Our Intelligence chaps were expecting something to materialize. After all every country occupied by the Boche organized a resistance group almost immediately.'

Outside it was beginning to get dark. In the corridor all was silent save for someone pecking inexpertly at a typewriter in the Duty Officer's room.

'Then we picked up this from the Nazi Party paper *Der Völkische Beobachter* last November. Just a little quote from a speech made to the German Home Guard by Himmler, but our people thought it significant.' He read the quote from a slip of paper on the desk. "'New resistance will spring up behind their backs," the Allies' backs, that is, "time and time again. And like werewolves, brave as death, volunteers will strike the enemy." But, as the months went by, nothing happened and Intelligence began to forget about the whole thing. They saw it as no more than one more attempt to pep up civilians with talk of wonder weapons and so on. That was until last month. On Palm Sunday six Germans – four SS men, a woman belonging to the Hitler Maidens and a sixteen-year-old boy belonging to the Hitler Youth movement – parachuted into the woods just west of Aachen on the German-Belgium border and worked their way into the town. At that time Aachen was the largest city in Germany in Allied hands, and it had an American-appointed burgo-master – a chap named Oppenhoff, Franz Oppenhoff. On the evening of Palm Sunday, they shot Oppenhoff dead at the door of his own house. Three weeks later the *Völkische Beobachter* announced that a traitor had been killed by German freedom-fighters. Two days later *Radio Werewolf* started operating from somewhere near Berlin and we knew that the first German resistance movement had been born, particularly when the station began broadcasting stuff like this:

"'Destroy the enemy or destroy yourself. Civilian or soldier, whether you are still un-occupied or deep behind enemy lines, fight on! Every burgomaster in Allied-held terri-tory is to be liquidated at the earliest pos-sible opportunity. Every Bolshevik, every Briton, every American found on German soil is our legitimate prey. In such cases, our movement does not need to take into account the conventions observed by the regular armed forces." As you can see, it's heady stuff that clearly appeals to the Boche soul.'

Crooke sucked his front teeth thought-fully. 'Possibly. But really I can't share your forebodings. Our chaps are on the River Elbe and Patton's men are already pushing into Bavaria. What if these fanatics do kill a

31

few odd dispatch riders or transport people? It's hard luck, but that's about all.'

'Let me show you something else.' Mallory rose and walked over to a big map of Central Europe hanging on the wall. He traced a line through Austria from the Swiss border into Northern Italy and back again into Bavaria in Germany. 'That rough circle,' he explained, 'covers about twenty thousand square miles of enemy-held territory and each of those symbols you can see indicates a new military installation  food dumps, petrol points, troops bunkers, underground factories – which have been located by the Air Force or our agents in these last couple of weeks since the Werewolf business started.' He picked up the piece of paper again. 'This is what the latest SHAEF intelligence summary had to say about the area. "Accumulated ground information and a limited amount of photo-graphic evidence now make it possible to give a rather more definite estimate of the progress of plans for the last-ditch stand of the Nazi Party... The main trend of German defence policy does seem directed primarily to the safeguarding of the Alpine Zone. Air cover shows at least twenty sites of recent underground activity as well as numerous natural caves, where ground sources have reported underground accommodation for stores and personnel. The existence of several reported underground factories has also been confirmed. In addition, several new barracks and hutted camps have been seen on air photographs, particularly around Innsbruck, Landeck and the Berghof."'

Mallory paused for a moment. 'Now listen to this bit and remember that General Strong, who prepared the intelligence summary, is not a man given to wild conclusions. He knows his business.' He looked down at the paper again. '"It thus appears that ground reports of extensive preparations for the accommodation of the German Maquis-to-be are not unfounded."'

Crooke frowned. 'I didn't realize the Germans still had the resources to be able to do that kind of thing.'

'They have. And that's not all. Daily they're shipping in thousands of the best troops they've got left – paras, ski troops, SS – the lot. Tough resourceful men who have got nothing to lose by fighting on and in some cases a lot to gain by doing so, especially the SS people. They're being accompanied by a lot of the big Nazi brass hats and their families. Dulles's OSS people in Berne have already located Himmler's wife in the area as well as Frau Bormann and her children. The Alpine Redoubt – that's the name SHAEF has given the area – is preparing for a long siege. More than that, however, it is obviously intended as a base of operations for the Werewolves.'

'How do the Destroyers come into it? What exactly would be our mission?'

'The Werewolf movement would present no danger whatsoever, if we had to deal with Germans of the calibre of SS General Pruetzmann, its nominal head. At the moment he's busy trying to save his hide by negotiating with our people in Sweden. The rabble of ex-Hitler Youth kids and teenage SS men he's got under his command in North Germany – perhaps five thousand in all could be dealt with easily. But a German resistance movement operating from the Alpine Redoubt is a different proposition altogether, especially when it's commanded by the Hawk.'

'The Hawk?'

'Yes, *Obersturmbannführer* Horst Habicht of the SS, nicknamed by his associates as the "Hawk" because his name, *Habicht*, means "hawk" in English and because of his somewhat unfortunate features. Apparently, he is not the Aryan type at all. Nature has been unkind to him.' Mallory opened a drawer of his desk, took out a small photograph and handed it to Crooke. 'Habicht,' he said.

It showed a tall, emaciated man in the black uniform of the *Allgemeine SS*, striding along a busy city street, briefcase in hand. 'Taken on his way to the HQ of the Reich's Main Security Office in the Prinz Albrecht

Strasse in 1940,' Mallory explained.

Crooke could see now why the SS colonel had got his name. His face was dominated by a huge beak of a nose: a massive abomination which would have been laughable on another man. But not on this one. No one would laugh at this man and live long.

Thoughtfully he handed the photograph back to Mallory who put it back in his drawer. 'The Pole who took that picture for us was arrested a month later. The Hawk conducted his cross-examination personally, if that's what one can call the torture he was put to. When the Hawk had finished with him, he was a broken man. His fingernails had gone and most of his teeth. They smashed his testicles too before they finally garrotted him.'

Crooke could not restrain a gasp of horror. 'The man must be an utter sadist!'

'I don't think so,' Mallory said. 'Just inhuman. A man who decides on a course of action and lets nothing stop him in the execution of that course. The Hawk was one of Heydrich's blue-eyed boys right from the start, you see. He took part in Operation Canned Goods in 1939 when the Boche faked a Polish attack on a German radio station as an excuse to start their invasion of that country. It was he who shot the concentration camp inmates the Boche planted on the scene as evidence, dressed in Polish uniforms.

'In '40 he took part in the Meuse bridge op when the Boche captured the key crossings into Belgium by marching a column of supposed German deserters guarded by gendarmes over the bridges there. Naturally both the deserters and the gendarmes were the Hawk's men. The Belgians guarding the crossings were taken by complete surprise. The Hawk naturally had the lot massacred in cold blood. Undoubtedly he had a good military reason for doing so. He always would.'

'What then?'

'In '42 he was in the Middle East, trying to break the British economy with fake five-pound notes which the Boche had forced concentration camp inmates to forge for them. A year later we spotted him in Persia when the SS were planning to assassinate the Big Three – Churchill, Stalin and Roosevelt – at their Tehran meeting in October of that year. Thereafter we lost him for a bit. One of our sources in Warsaw reported that he had been captured by the Russians outside the Polish capital, but he must have been mistaken, because the Hawk turned up again last month as Pruetzmann's personal representative in command of the Werewolf in southern Germany. Dulles reported from Berne that there's no doubt about it: the Hawk is the man who is running the Werewolf in the Alpine Redoubt.'

'I see,' said Crooke. 'And our task?'

'The Destroyers' mission? To break into the Alpine Redoubt without delay and kill the Hawk!'

# FOUR

Colonel Stevens tapped the three-tonner's bonnet with his swagger cane. 'Still as good as new,' he said in his clipped Sandhurst voice. 'If I had my way, Jones, I'd run 'em for another fifty thousand miles. But those chairborne warriors at the War Office think differently.' He stroked his trim moustache, taking care not to dislodge it; the glue wasn't too good. 'Still, Jones, the army's loss is your gain, what?'

The little Yorkshire businessman beamed. 'Ay, it'd look like it, Colonel.'

Out of the corner of his eye Stevens could see the businessman's greedy little eyes sizing up the huge vehicle park of three-ton trucks with the white Y sign of the Fifth Division. Tomorrow the RASC drivers would be coming from the depot to take them down to the docks for shipping to the Continent where the Fifth, which had just been transferred from Italy to Germany, was anxiously waiting for its vehicles. Stevens knew he'd have to pull the deal off now or never.

'Sergeant,' he snapped to the dark-skinned NCO standing at the door of the olive-drab Chevrolet staff car 'borrowed' from outside the US headquarters in Grosvenor Square without the owner's consent, 'get up in one of those lorries and start her up.'

As the NCO hurried forward to carry out his order, he turned to the businessman and explained, 'They've been here like this for over two months now. Give you an idea of the quality of the goods you're buying.'

The NCO swung himself up behind the big wheel of the lorry which he and the 'Colonel' had worked on two hours earlier to ensure that its engine, not used since the vehicle had been shipped from Italy the month before, would start immediately.

'Is he a darkie?' Jones asked, as the NCO

fumbled with the ignition.

Colonel Stevens nodded. 'Yes, a wog. But a good chap all the same. Claims he's British, of course, but the tarbrush has been at work there somewhere or other.'

'Ay, looks like it to me,' Jones agreed.

Inside the truck, Gippo pressed the ignition button. The engine burst into life immediately. He revved it up for a moment and then took his foot off the accelerator. The engine ran sweetly and without trouble; their dickering with the motor that morning was paying dividends.

Jones was impressed. 'Sounds good to me, Colonel. Always tell a decent well-looked-after engine by the exhaust smoke. Nice and blue, not a bit o'black anywhere in it.' He sucked his teeth and put on what he liked to think was his shrewd canny Yorkshire businessman's face. 'But what's the catch, Colonel?'

'*Catch?*' Colonel Stevens OBE, late of the Rifle Brigade, now relegated to the ranks of the RASC since his wound in Normandy (or so he had told Jones), looked at the fat Yorkshireman as if he had just crawled out of the woodwork of the shed behind them. 'What the devil do you mean, sir?'

Jones held up his hands conciliatorily. 'No offence, Colonel. But I mean to say, you're offering them as war surplus at twenty quid a piece. I think they're worth a bit more. Say thirty.' In the back of his mind he was already selling them to his pals in Leeds and Bradford, starved of new or even decent second-hand vehicles since 1939, for at least three hundred. 'What I can't figure out, yer see, is why you don't auction them off. You'd get more 'happen.'

'Doubt it,' Stevens said. 'Dealers' rings make a fortune keeping the prices down by agreement. Chaps in the War Office know what they're doing on that score at least. Twenty pounds per vehicle it is. Now then, Jones, I'm a busy man. How many are you going to take? Cash in advance naturally.'

'Naturally,' Jones said hastily, not wishing to offend the strange colonel again. This could be his first really big post-war deal. 'What about fifty?'

Stevens gave him a hard little smile. 'Fifty or five hundred – it makes no difference to me, Jones. I'm not one of you businessmen chappies, always out to make a turn. Just a simple soldier.'

'Simple soldier, of course,' Jones echoed the words and produced a massive roll of notes.

'That's the ticket,' Stevens said. 'Fifty times twenty. If my maths serve me rightly, that'll be a thousand pounds.'

Jones licked his thumb and began to count out the five-pound notes carefully. Over his bent head, Stevens looked at the NCO's greedy face and winked. Gippo winked back. Casually Colonel Stevens stowed them away in the pocket of his well-cut British warm coat and smacked his swagger cane against his leg. 'Well, Jones, that's that, I suppose. Just one thing.'

'What's that, Colonel?'

'I've to get back to London in somewhat

of a hurry. Conference at the War Office, you know. Wonder if you would take care of painting the "sold" sign on the lorries? My driver will give you the gear.'

'Of course, Colonel. Be only too glad to save your chap the trouble,' Jones said eagerly, 'though I don't believe in being soft with darkies.'

Minutes later, as the two Destroyers drove away in the 'borrowed' staff car, he was happily engaged stencilling 'sold' on the first vehicle, while a tousle-haired mechanic stared out of the dirty window of the shed at the strange civvy in bewildered silence.

'The silly sod would never have fallen for it if he hadn't been so bleedin' greedy,' Colonel Stevens was saying when two redcaps on motorcycles flashed by them, swung inwards and forced Gippo to jam on the brakes. The Destroyers did not panic; they were used to this sort of thing. While the two MPs advanced towards them, Stevens jammed the thick wad of fivers down the back of the seat behind him.

The bigger of the two came level with the window at Stevens' side. His chest was covered with ribbons. Stevens spotted the Africa Star among them. The corporal would be nobody's fool; he'd been around. Still Stevens was not prepared to give in without a fight. 'I say, Corporal,' he snapped angrily, reverting to his 'officer and gentleman's voice', 'what the devil do you think you're at? You could have damn well run us into the ditch. Look at my chap here.'

The redcap was not impressed. 'Belt up,' he said laconically. 'You Stevens?'

'*Colonel* Stevens!'

'Colonel my arse,' the redcap said. 'We've been after you ever since London.'

Stevens grinned up at the MP cheekily. When he spoke again his voice had reverted to its normal cockney. 'Are yer gonna pinch us, corp?'

'No, yer sodding well lucky this time.' He jerked his thumb back the way they had come. 'You two lags is wanted back at the

Admiralty at once. Urgent conference or something.' He pulled down his goggles again. 'So get yer finger out and turn that fancy car that you've half-inched round and get on the way to London. We'll take yer in.'

Stevens turned to Gippo, who claimed that he was the illegitimate descendant of Lord Kitchener, though before the war he had worked at Port Said selling porno-graphic pictures to tourists off the cruise liners, and said in his colonel's voice, 'Be a good chap and turn round. The First Lord wants to see me urgently.'

Gippo crashed home the gear and said two very rude words.

Mallory and the rest of the Destroyers were waiting for them in the Admiral's office, Room 38, when they arrived at the Admir-alty. Leaning against the cream-coloured walls or squatting on the iron radiators they observed their running mates' entrance without comment: Thaelmann, the hard-bitten German communist who had escaped from Dachau concentration camp just after the Nazi takeover and had fought against fascism ever since; Lone Star Alamo Jones, the absurdly named Texan mercenary; a yellow-faced heartless killer, know to the rest of the team as 'Yank'; and Peters, the big, bluff ex-company sergeant major in the Coldstream Guards.

Stevens looked at them cheekily, then gave his casual senior officer's salute, touching his red-banded staff cap with the tip of his swagger cane. 'Good of you chaps to wait for us,' he said and took a seat in the one comfortable leather armchair.

'Stevens,' Crooke said warningly. 'Remember you're still in the army.'

'Not for much longer, sir,' the cockney answered airily. 'Demob group twenty-five, that's me. Two months more and the Kate Karney'll have to do without the services of Private Stevens.'

'All right, that's enough,' Mallory said. 'And, by the way, *Colonel* Stevens, I'll have that thousand pounds from you at the end of this conference. I suppose someone has to protect fools like that.' He held his hand up to stop any protest. 'Later. Now let's get on with it.' Swiftly he sketched in the situation in Germany, repeating very much the same explanation he had given Crooke the night before. The Destroyers listened in attentive silence, but Mallory could see that they did not like what they heard. He finished his description of the Alpine Redoubt and the role Intelligence thought the Hawk would play in it and then nodded to Crooke.

Crooke tugged at his eye patch and looked at the hard faces of the men he had commanded these last two and a half years since he had offered them their freedom from long prison sentences in return for service in the Destroyers. Something was wrong. He didn't know what, but he had served long enough with these men whom Brooke had characterized as the 'scum of the British Army' to sense that they didn't like the idea of a new mission. 'Well, you've heard what Commander Mallory has had to say and I'm sure you realize that this country cannot afford another year of war. Something has to be done...' He stopped lamely, seeing the complete lack of enthusiasm in their eyes.

'You mean, sir, you expect us Destroyers to stick our sodding necks out yet again,' Stevens said coldly, 'and do this Hawk bloke in? That's it, isn't it?'

Crooke nodded.

'Well, I don't like it, sir.'

'Why?'

'Why? Because I think we've done enough, Commander. Me and Gippo wants to get started up in business before everybody gets demobbed.'

'Monkey business no doubt,' Mallory said.

But Stevens' serious look didn't change. 'You wait till groups twenty-six and twenty-seven get out. They'll flood the market with their labour. It'll be like 1919 all over again. Me and Gippo wants to get our hands on the pickings before then.'

'Now, come on, Stevens,' Mallory tried to humour him. 'There's going to be a bright new socialist world after the war. What about the Beveridge Plan, the emergency training scheme, retraining schemes, gratuities – the lot.'

'Pie in the sky!' Stevens said scornfully. 'All right if yer want to be some sodding little council school teacher waiting a hundred years for your piddling little pension. But me and Gippo wants to get into the big time. I mean it's all right for you, Commander. You've been to that posh school of yours and you're in the right clubs and that. You're quids in. But working class fellers like us have to work at it – put in some real hard graft.'

Mallory looked at Crooke in surprise.

Crooke turned to the others. 'What do the rest of you think?'

There was silence until Peters spoke for them. 'Ever since our lads crossed the Rhine, sir,' he said in the polite regular soldier's manner of his, 'we've talked about it a lot –

what we're going to do after demob. Thaelmann is going back to Germany. Yank's off to the Pacific, and I'm going to apply for one of the government retraining schemes Commander Mallory mentioned.'

'You mean you're leaving the army, too, Peters?' Crooke exclaimed. 'But you're a regular.'

'That's right, sir. But my time's up and there's no future for me in the army.'

'Don't you understand, sir?' Steven butted in. 'We've had it! There's no future in the Destroyers for us. The lot of us want to be civvies again, as soon as poss. It's as simple as that.'

Mallory looked at Crooke, aghast. 'But you can't *do* this,' he said. 'You're still in the army.'

'We *can*, Commander,' Stevens retorted. 'Nobody can force us to go to Germany again and risk our necks on some sodding last mission. Let some of the young 'uns go, who haven't got their knees brown yet. The Destroyers have had a bellyful.'

For a moment Crooke did not speak. Then he broke the silence. 'I could appeal to your patriotism. I could tell you that the British Empire will soon undergo the most serious crisis of its whole three-hundred-year-old history, in spite of the fact that this country has won a great victory. I could point out that we have fought together for nearly three years now and have been through some pretty tough times together in Africa, Russia and Italy. But I won't do that.' He paused and looked around the semi-circle of tough, attentive faces. 'Your attitude leaves me one alternative only, to remind you of the way you were recruited to the Destroyers!' He could see by the looks in their eyes that they had not forgotten that burning hot day in the Cairo glasshouse just before El Alamein when he had had them fetched out of the 'tank' and promised them their freedom if they would join him in the new unit. 'I see you remember,' he said. 'All of you were released to me personally. But I'd like to point out that you hadn't served out your sentences. You, Stevens, for desertion. You, Yank, for murder. You, Thaelmann, for treachery. You, Gippo, for...'

'You wouldn't do that, sir!' Stevens cut him short, his face suddenly deathly pale. 'You *couldn't!*'

'I could, Stevens,' Crooke said. 'You must understand, all of you, that there are forces at work in this country which could destroy the work of three hundred years if we don't fight against them. The British Empire could be destroyed as easily as that.' He snapped his fingers. 'This war must be brought to an end as swiftly as possible if we are going to counter those forces and save the Empire. Then we shall be able to root out the traitors in our own ranks, the office-seekers, the intellectual appeasers and all the rest of those parlour pinks who want to give away the Empire our forefathers fought and died for. In the light of the enormity of that problem, our personal fates are of little importance. The war in Europe must be brought to a close within the next four weeks and

Operation Werewolf will play an important role in the achievement of that end. Whether you men like it or not, we are flying out to General Patton's Third Army for further briefing tomorrow morning.'

'Christ on a crutch!' the Yank said, half in anger, half in admiration. 'You're a hard bastard, Crooke!'

There was no admiration in Stevens' voice, just anger. 'But how do you know you can rely on us – sir – when you're alone with us?'

Crooke looked at him for a moment before he spoke. He touched the revolver at his side, a faint smile flickered on his lips but there was no answering light in his eye. 'You mean with my back to you, Stevens? You've got to catch me first, haven't you?'

Mallory's heart sank. Operation Werewolf was getting started on one hell of a bad note.

# FIVE

General Patton's Third Army HQ in a former Wehrmacht barracks at Bad Hersfeld near Frankfurt was like an armed camp. Helmeted sentries carrying grease guns were everywhere. Two armoured cars were posted in the courtyard of the headquarters building and even the clerks wore their helmet liners and had .45s slung round their stomachs.

Mallory, accompanied by Crooke and the Destroyers, looked at Colonel Oscar Koch, Patton's intelligence officer.

'Werewolf,' Koch answered his unspoken question. 'Our agents have warned us to expect a gliderborne attack at any moment. Even the General's been sleeping with his pistols under his pillow these last few nights!'

They passed into Koch's office.

'Take a seat, fellers,' he said in an easy manner, and he handed Mallory a sheet of paper. 'Just came in from SHAEF this morning. Typical of the whole goddam Werewolf scare, if you ask me.'

Mallory surveyed it quickly and then read it aloud. 'Your attitude towards women in Germany is wrong. Do you know that German women have been trained to seduce you? Is it worth a knife in the back? A weapon can be concealed by women on the chest, between the breasts, on the abdomen, on the upper leg, under the buttocks… How can you search women? The answer to that one is difficult. It may be your life at stake. You may find a weapon by forcing them to pull their dress tight against their bodies here and there. If it is a small object you are hunting for, you must have another woman to do the searching and do it thoroughly in a private room.'

Koch chuckled. 'Would you believe it! What kind of jerk must have written that kind of crap? He mustn't have been close to

56

a battlefield in his whole goddam life. A private room – my aching back!'

Mallory smiled, but the Destroyers' faces remained impassive. He glanced at Crooke. Did the Destroyers' CO know what he was doing, he wondered, forcing them to go on this mission when they had no heart for it? Could Crooke rely on them in a tight corner now? But if Crooke was worried, his face revealed nothing of those worries.

Mallory turned back to Koch. 'Colonel, I wonder if you could brief my chaps on what you know and how they are to get through the Boche lines.'

'Okay, this is what we know from Dulles in Switzerland – he's keeping a close eye on the Alpine Redoubt situation. Your man – this guy Habicht – is holed up in Schloss Hoellenthal, just on the other side of the German border in Austria. Tough nut to crack as far as we know.'

'How do you mean, Colonel?' Crooke asked.

'Well, from the little bit of info that

Dulles's agents have been able to get out of the Redoubt, Schloss Hoellenthal is an old Hapsburg hunting lodge which the Krauts have fortified intensively over the last couple of months. If that weren't bad enough, it's perched on a mountain top with clear fields of fire on all sides. The Hawk's looking after himself, believe you me. It'll be no walkover, that's for sure.'

Hurriedly Mallory changed the subject. He didn't want the Destroyers' morale lowered any further. 'We'll worry about that detail later. How are these chaps going to make a start on the mission?'

'That's no problem. The front's pretty fluid. If it weren't for this goddam Werewolf scare, we'd barrel through the Krauts like a dose of salts down here in Bavaria. But SHAEF is urging caution and we've got to obey orders. My suggestion is that your guys go up with one of our recon teams – say with the Fourth Armoured Division – and then slip across into Kraut country wherever they can find a gap for you.'

Crooke and Mallory considered the information for a moment. 'But time's short and we've got a lot of country to cover, Colonel,' Crooke said. 'How are we going to pinpoint our man quickly?'

'That's no problem. We've got three OSS teams in this part of the world, behind the Kraut lines – Jedburghs, we call them. I propose that your – er – Destroyers contact the B team located in Nuremberg.'

'The B team?' Mallory queried.

'Yeah. It's the usual three man set-up the OSS use. There's a Czech radio operator, a former Kraut POW who volunteered to fight for us when he was in the cage. Says he's always been an anti-Nazi. That's what they all say these days – now they're losing out. And there's Major Falk – fluent German speaker and former college prof, among other things.'

'What do you mean?' Crooke asked, sensing that Koch was not altogether too happy about Major Falk.'

'Oh, nothing.'

'I must insist, Colonel,' Crooke said firmly. 'I can't risk my men's lives in any way. Our mission is tricky enough. If you've any doubts, I'd be grateful if you'd let me know *now*.'

'I guess my slip must be showing,' Koch said. 'But I've never liked Falk much. He worked for me and the general in Africa before he volunteered for the OSS. I got to know him out there and what I saw I didn't like.'

'Anything specific?'

'Well, I'm not a rabid Republican like General Patton, but I've never gone much on the Democrats. Falk – he calls himself a Roosevelt New Dealer. Okay, that wouldn't worry me under normal circumstances – I can take the average New Dealer without too much pain. But Falk is more than that. In my honest opinion, gentlemen, Falk is nothing other than a goddam commie!'

'Gentlemen,' a soft Slavic voice broke in.

They turned, startled, towards the door. A squat, shaven-headed officer in the earth-coloured blouse and dark breeches of the Red Army stood there, smiling at them with a mouthful of gleaming, stainless-steel teeth. Huge glittering epaulettes decorated his massive shoulders. 'Did I hear the word communist?'

Koch flushed. 'I was just talking in general terms, Colonel Petrov,' he blustered. Hurriedly he waved a hand at the Destroyers. 'These men belong to the British Naval Intelligence's famous Destroyer squad. You might have heard of them?'

The Russian colonel smiled at the Destroyers, but his eyes were cold and calculating. 'Of course. The celebrated Destroyers. I have heard that you were in the Soviet Union a couple of years ago, yes?'

'Yes,' Crooke said coldly. Instinctively he disliked the squat Mongolian-looking Red Army man. He added no further information about their mission behind the Russian lines in 1943. There was a moment's awkward silence. Then the Russian laughed with faked joviality. 'I was wanting to talk to you,

Colonel Koch,' he said. 'But it can wait till later. I shall come back when you are finished with the famous Destroyers.' He touched his big paw to his shaven skull. 'Good afternoon, gentlemen.' Koch did not say anything until he was sure that the Russian had left the corridor outside. 'Russian liaison team,' he explained. 'At least officially.'

'What do you mean?' Mallory asked.

'That's his official function. My guess is that he's the NKVD's rep at Third Army headquarters – or perhaps Russian Military Intelligence's. But whatever he is, I, for one, wouldn't trust Colonel Petrov as far as I could throw him.' He dropped the subject. 'All right, gentlemen, that's the deal. The Fourth'll slip you through the Kraut lines and you'll make your way to Nuremberg. There you'll contact Falk and he'll brief you further. From there on in I guess you'll have to play it by ear.'

'Thank you, Colonel.' Mallory rose to his feet. The Destroyers followed suit. 'With your permission I'll get my chaps kitted out for the mission now.'

Colonel Koch waved a soft hand at him. 'Not just yet, Commander, if you don't mind. The general would like to meet your chaps again and he can't stand people in civilian clothes.'

'You mean General Patton?'

'Yes. He has been very impressed by your previous work. Now he wants to give you a private briefing.'

Crooke looked at Mallory in amazement. Ever since the Destroyers had been formed, the brass had had very little time for them. To most of the generals they had dealt with in these last three years, the Destroyers had been a necessary evil, nothing more. 'Stone the crows,' Stevens said cynically, 'we ain't half coming up in the world, ain't we!' His voice rose nastily. '"The general has been very impressed by our previous work." Ain't that just ducky!'

'Shut up, Stevens,' Crooke snapped and, turning to a puzzled Koch, he asked: 'Where do we meet the general, Colonel Koch?'

'Where?' he echoed Crooke's question. 'Unfortunately at a place which is calculated to make you sick to your stomach. It did mine yesterday just after our boys had captured it – Ohrdruf Concentration Camp.'

# SIX

Ohrdruf – a row of ugly wooden barracks surrounded by a double enclosure of barbed wire – was like a nasty wound in the middle of the lovely spring countryside. Even before the Destroyers' truck pulled up behind the convoy of staff cars outside the entrance the stench of death hit them.

In shocked silence, their fingers gripping their noses to keep out the smell, the Destroyers jumped from the truck and stared at the brown wooden huts and the human skeletons in their tattered striped pyjamas who crawled about the compound which was littered with human waste.

'My God,' Mallory gasped. 'I never thought it would be this bad.'

'Come on,' Crooke said. 'Let's find the general.' It was almost as if he was experiencing some kind of perverted pleasure from inflicting this scene on his men.

'Blood an' Guts? He's in Hut 47,' a driver, with a khaki handkerchief tied across his mouth, said thickly.

Inside the compound the agony of the inmates showed itself clearly in their expressions. With their eyes sunken and listless and too weak to close their mouths, they extended their matchstick-thin arms as the Destroyers hurried by and cried weakly: *'Essen – bitte Essen!'* Just as they reached Hut 47, one of the living skeletons in front of them collapsed. His sole garment – a shirt which was much too big for him – fell open to reveal the concentration camp number tattooed on to the inside of his emaciated, scabby thigh. Slowly, painfully, two other former prisoners picked him up by his ankles and shoulders and began to lug him back to his barracks.

General Patton, the tall, immaculately dressed Commander of the US Third Army, was accompanied by the Allied Supreme

Commander in Europe, General Eisenhower, as he came out of the stinking Hut 47 in which the inmates slept three in a bunk, with the wooden beds ranging six on top of one another right up to the ceiling. His usual pugnacious scowl was absent.

Under his gleaming, lacquered helmet with its three gold stars, his long face was pale. Eisenhower was equally white, the wide mouthed grin replaced by a look of horror and disgust at what they had just seen.

The two senior officers recognized the Destroyers standing stiffly at attention and nodded. Patton opened his mouth to say something, but he never managed to get the words out. Abruptly he turned, broke away from the party, strode swiftly to the back of the hut and was sick.

'Excuse me, General,' Patton said, as he came back, wiping his mouth with an elegant silk handkerchief. 'Couldn't help myself.'

'That's all right,' Eisenhower said, 'I feel like that myself. You okay now?'

Patton nodded, not trusting himself to speak.

'All right, let's get out of this place.'

The party made its way back to the entrance, past the half-filled, still smoking ovens of the crematorium. In front of them a pile of thirty or forty naked corpses were stacked, criss-crossed like matches and about as substantial. Following behind the Destroyers looked at them, their tough bronzed faces suddenly pale, reflecting their overwhelming horror. Thaelmann, usually so unemotional, was crying openly.

As they stood at the entrance to the camp under its mocking cynical sign *Arbeit Macht Frei*, waiting for the staff cars to draw up, Patton turned to Mallory and said, 'You and the other officer come in my vehicle. I need to talk to you.'

Just then one of the GIs who had liberated the camp bumped into an ex-Nazi guard, his face puffed up and swollen where the enraged Third Army men had beaten him. From sheer nerves he began to giggle.

General Eisenhower turned at the absurd sound in this place of absolute horror. He looked at the young soldier coldly and when he finally spoke to him, his every word was like the drop off an icicle. 'Still having trouble hating them?' he asked. The GI lowered his eyes.

Eisenhower raised his voice so that all the assembled brass and the GI onlookers could hear. 'I want every American unit not in the front line to see this place,' he said. 'We are told that the American soldier does not know what he is fighting for. Now, at least, he will know what he is fighting *against*.'

Just behind him Stevens lowered his eyes to the ground, as if he were suddenly ashamed.

Then they drove away, leaving the stench of dysentery, despair and death behind them. Patton sat next to his chief aide, Colonel Charles Codman, facing Mallory and Crooke, staring grimly at nothing. Then he pulled out a long cigar and lit it fussily.

He breathed out a thin stream of smoke

and said slowly, 'That's better, though I doubt I shall be able ever to get the stench of that place out of my nostrils.' He looked at the two British officers opposite him. 'But then perhaps,' he added softly, 'we're not meant to, eh?'

Mallory nodded.

'Gentlemen,' Patton went on, 'what you have just seen is horrible, terrible – there aren't enough adjectives in Webster's Dictionary to describe that place. But Ohrdruf belongs to the past. We have destroyed the monsters who created it. Now we are faced by another monster, which is equally terrible.'

'What do you mean, sir?' Crooke asked.

'What do I mean?' he repeated Crooke's question. 'The Russians, our erstwhile Allies.'

'No, General,' Codman admonished softly.

'Hell, you know I'm right, Charley,' Patton snorted. 'We're going to have to fight them sooner or later. Within the next generation. Why not do it now while our army is intact and the damn Russians can have their hind end kicked back into Russia in three months? We can do it easily.'

'General – *please*,' Codman urged. 'I don't think you should say such things.' His voice rose.

But Patton refused to shut up. 'What do I care? I'd like to get the war started with them right now. If those creeps at SHAEF would give me just ten days, I could have enough incidents happen to have us at war with those sons of bitches and make it look like their fault. Then we'd be completely justified in attacking them and running them out.'

'What exactly do you mean, General?' Mallory asked, in an effort to humour him.

'What do I mean? I mean that the Russians intend to grab the whole of Central Europe. It's obvious they're going to take Berlin, while our men are sitting on their fat asses on the Elbe because Ike has ordered them not to advance any further. They'll grab Vienna too – that's for sure. And what the commies grab they keep, believe you me. That Stalin is a bastard, just as mean and ruthless as Hitler.

He might have made polite noises at Yalta about freedom of expression and elections in the territories overrun by the Red Army. But every country the Russians take over will remain communist after the war, you can have my word on that. But goddamit, I'm not going to give them Prague and Czechoslovakia!'

'How do you mean, sir?'

'I've got six hundred thousand tough trained soldiers in my army. The biggest army in US military history. Those guys could take Prague and the rest of the country – just like that.' He clicked his fingers aggressively. 'But there's that goddam Alpine Redoubt in the way. My instinct is to go for Prague like hell. But Ike has other ideas. He wants me to attack the Alpine Redoubt first.'

They passed a column of towed 5.5s. The coloured gunners took off their helmets and waved them as they recognized Patton.

The general faked another smile and waved back, but there was no enthusiasm in the gesture. Wearily he sat back against the padded leather seat.

Mallory realized that the commander around whom the Press had woven the gory legend of hard-drinking, hard-living, aggressive profanity these last couple of years was really a tired old man.

As the car began to slow down and the first modern blocks of Hersfeld, pocked here and there by machine-gun fire, came into view, Patton sighed wearily and said, 'Commander, see to it that your Destroyers get this Redoubt business cleared up – and quick. Time is running out for me, my army, for the whole Western world. You understand? Time is running out for us. Now the advantage is with the commies.'

Mallory nodded.

Three hours later the Destroyers' truck began to pull away from the HQ towards the setting sun. For a moment or two Mallory stood in the courtyard watching them go. He did not wave. Nor did the Destroyers sitting in the back. They stared at him in silence.

Then the truck turned the corner and was gone. For a moment Mallory stood there alone, deep in thought. Then he turned and made his way back inside.

Up above, at the window of his office on the second floor, Colonel Petrov waiting till Mallory had disappeared from view and pulled down the blinds.

'Piotr,' he snapped.

His second-in-command, a tall, skinny captain with one arm and with two Red Stars on his blouse, hurried to the door and locked it. He pulled out his pistol and posted himself there. The colonel waited till he had done so. '*Horascho,*' he said, satisfied that their security was all right.

He sat down at the desk under the window, flicked on the lamp and took the covers off their transmitter. Slipping on the headphones, he took out the encoded message and laid it on the table on his left side. He moved the morse key a couple of times to check if it was working correctly. He turned on the power and began to send

74

a message. In spite of his sausage-like fingers, Colonel Petrov had a nice speed.

At the door the one-armed captain of the NKVD nodded his head in approval; but he did not attempt to follow the morse. He knew what the message contained anyway. He had encoded it himself two hours before when Petrov had discovered what the British provocateurs' mission was. It was simple. Reduced to its basic element, it read, 'Liquidate the Destroyers!'

# SEVEN

Moonlight flooded the cobbled Bavarian road. Up ahead a pink glow tinged the clouds. On both sides the shelled fields were filled with the long shadows of the waiting Sherman tanks and white scout cars. Somewhere a Spandau machine gun was chattering rapidly and white and red tracer zig-zagged through the night. But the enemy fire and the prospect of dangerous action did not seem to worry the veterans of the Fighting Fourth; the leather-helmeted tankers and their squad of armoured infantry had been through this sort of thing time and time again in these last nine months since their had first gone into action in Brittany. It was not for nothing that the Division's unofficial motto was: 'Hell, they've got us surrounded again – the poor bastards!'

Smoking quietly in the pre-dawn chill, their hands carefully cupped around the glowing ends of their cigarettes, the Destroyers listened to the soft chatter around them, as they waited for the signal to move out. Colonel Creighton Abrams had given them the best recon team he had in his whole combat command at Patton's express order and if anyone could get them through the German lines it was them.

'Sir.' It was Stevens.

'Yes, Stevens?'

'Well, it's about what we said in London, sir,' he said. 'That we've had a bellyful and all that, like,' he broke off lamely.

'Yes?' Crooke prompted.

'Well, while you was at the "O" group with that Yank officer, sir, me and the lads had a little bit of a chat about what happened this afternoon.'

'You mean at the camp?'

'Yes, that's right. Well, sir, we decided to take back what we said in London – you know what I mean. After this afternoon,' he

78

shrugged, 'what *we* all want to do don't really seem much important.'

At the head of the column a Patton tank burst into noisy life. A cloud of blue smoke shot from its exhaust. On its turret the young captain waved his arm around in a rapid circle – the signal to mount up. 'All right, you guys,' Sergeant Cooper, the huge hulking platoon sergeant in charge of the white half-track in which they were going to travel, bellowed above the noise as engine after engine burst into action. 'Or do you limeys take a cup of tea before you go into combat?'

'You know what you can do, buddy?' Yank snarled, as they clambered up the steel-plated side, and dropped down among the crouching, heavily armed infantry.

'Yeah, and you too,' Cooper snapped back, 'and your mother as well!'

There was a clatter of tracks. The lead tank began to move off. One by one the rest of the column followed. Up ahead the German lines were still silent and foreboding, but

Crooke, squatting next to Sergeant Cooper, who clutched his MI rifle in his big dirty paws grimly, did not notice the heavy menace that permeated the night air. His mind was still full of what had just happened. The Destroyers were a unified team once more. Nothing could stop them now – the Werewolf movement or any other damn thing that the Hawk cared to throw at them. Now the Destroyers could not help but win through!

Just as the pre-dawn sky began to break up into the dirty white which heralded the morning, the young captain in charge of the Fourth's recon team lead the column off the cobbled road on to a rough bumpy dirt track that ran off at an angle.

'We're gonna swing round the roadblock the Krauts has further up,' Cooper explained as the walkie-talkie at his side began to crackle.

By pressing his face close to Cooper's unshaven jowl, Crooke could hear the captain's distorted unreal voice. 'Hello G-6,' he called, 'Kraut village two klicks further up. The cans' – he used the code word for the tanks – 'will go up first. The soft-skinned vehicles'll follow. Over.'

'Roger and out,' Cooper grunted and put the walkie-talkie down again. 'Okay, you guys,' he yelled at the armoured infantry, 'get ready to haul ass, if the Krauts hit us!'

The soldiers who had been dozing fitfully in the back of the half-track took up their carbines and MIs and took up their positions on both sides, eyeing the pine woods that bordered the narrow track warily. The Destroyers, armed with their borrowed US grease guns, did the same. They crawled closer and closer to the German village, but nothing happened. The woods gave way to open fields. In front of them on a slight rise the typical onion-shaped steeple of a baroque southern German church loomed up. Around it the bulky shapes of the first wooden houses came into view. Nothing stirred. Not even a village dog barked. If the village were still occupied, its inhabitants had obviously hidden themselves deep in the cellars below the houses.

'Hello, hello, George Six... We're approaching the first house.' It was the young captain. 'Let the cans come on up now!'

Cooper thumped the driver on the shoulder and indicated he should slow down even further. As the tanks rumbled by, the white half-track slowed down to a walking pace. Crooke rose to his feet behind the big .5-inch machine gun mounted on the stanchion behind the driver and watched them go in from two different angles, following the lead of the captain's big new Patton. Cautiously, their big 75mm cannon swinging from side to side, they rumbled closer and closer to the church. Still nothing moved in the village.

Cooper pushed back his helmet to reveal a mop of curly black hair. He wiped the sweat off his brow. 'Ah,' he sighed, 'looks as if the Krauts has bugged out after all...'

He was stopped by a soft crump coming

from a big white-painted barn next to the church.

'Hot shit!' he yelled, 'a *panzerfaust!*'

The next moment came the echoing boom of metal striking metal. The lead Patton came to a halt. An orange-yellow flame shot thirty feet into the sky. The turret was thrown open and a screaming figure clutched at the red-hot metal, trying desperately to escape the inferno.

A ragged crackle of rifle-fire erupted from the line of houses. A machine gun started to chatter, sending a stream of tracer towards the tanks. A stick grenade sailed from a shattered window. It exploded on the tank's turret. The young captain disappeared from view.

'The rotten sons-of-bitches!' Cooper yelled and, lifting his MI, he fired a wild burst at the line of houses.

It seemed to act as a signal for the rest. All along the column the armoured infantry began to blaze away at their unseen opponents, while the tanks tried to back away under a cloud of white smoke. But now the *panzerfaust* bombs were exploding among the Shermans everywhere. They were sitting ducks, outlined as they were against the glare of the burning Patton.

The first Sherman was hit and came to an abrupt halt. Another was hit in its most sensitive spot, near the gasoline engine. It went up in flames immediately, its exploding ammunition zig-zagging into the sky at a crazy angle. But as they backed down the hill, the remaining three continued to fire valiantly into the village.

The barn from which the first *panzerfaust* bomb had been fired crashed in ruins. A house was hit and began to burn furiously. Everything now was frenzied confusion, with the half-track drivers trying to turn their vehicles round in the narrow track, while they were still covered by the retreating tanks.

But the German ambush had been well planned. Suddenly lead pattered against the side of their White like heavy rain. Crooke ducked. Next to him Cooper clutched his shoulder and cursed. His MI clattered to the deck. Blood started to pour through his fingers. 'The bastards have winged me,' he cried, his face a deathly white. 'Get this goddam thing out of here.'

His words were drowned by the explosion of a stick grenade below the front axle. The White lurched to a stop. Over Cooper's shoulder Crooke caught a glimpse of a boyish face behind a tree twenty yards away. He fired and the face disappeared. Now he saw that there were other youthful faces hidden in the fields on both sides.

'Bale out!' he yelled. *'Quick.'*

The armoured infantrymen needed no urging. While Crooke grabbed the .5-inch machine gun and sprayed the field to their front, they swung themselves over the sides, pressing their bodies close to the edge so that they would present the smallest possible target.

Gippo was about to follow them, but Crooke yelled at him to stay where he was.

Beyond the dead driver, slumped over the wheel, the engine was beginning to burn. Thick white smoke was drifting towards them. Crooke fired another wild burst to give the infantry in the field a chance to double to the nearest cover, then he pushed Cooper to the floor. With a groan Cooper sank to his knees. 'Stay there, Sergeant,' he yelled above the crazy roar. 'Even if the engine goes up.'

He ducked as a burst of lead cut the air all about them. 'All right, you Destroyers,' he cried. 'We're getting the hell out of here! By ourselves!'

'But we can't abandon the Yanks!' Peters yelled, his face lathered in sweat in the ruddy glow from the burning tanks.

'Oh yes, we can. Our lives are more important than theirs! *Come on!*'

Not giving them chance to argue further, he dropped over the other side of the half-track. As he fell to the hard ground, he sprayed the area with his grease gun. There was an agonized scream of pain, but he could not identify its source. He began to double towards the village. 'Follow me,' he yelled, firing from the hip.

In a ragged line they ran after him up the slope.

A long-haired youth in leather shorts, who didn't look a day over fourteen, sprang up from behind a pile of firewood. In his hand he clutched a stick grenade. The Yank let him have a burst in the stomach. He screamed and sprawled forward, a long lock of blond hair dangling over his forehead.

Another leather-shorted boy tried to grab Peters. The ex-sergeant-major brought the metal base of his grease gun up under the lad's chin. As he doubled up, screaming with pain, Gippo kicked him neatly in the seat of his *Lederhosen.*

Crooke ran on. He knew he was taking a terrible risk. But he knew too from past experience that to head right into the heart of an attack was often the best way out of an ambush. The enemy did not expect that kind of a reaction.

They doubled past the burning Patton. Two black-jacketed youths in short pants tried to bar their way, Schmeisser machine pistols held across their chests. A burst from Thaelmann's grease gun bowled them over. 'God almighty,' he yelled, as he sprang over their bodies. 'They're just schoolkids!'

They ran into the cobbled street. A big brown horse broke out of the burning barn to their right, squealing with terror. A couple of lumbering oxen followed it.

'Behind them,' Crooke yelled desperately. *'Behind the animals!'*

They reacted immediately. The crazed animals blundered head-first into the hastily erected roadblock which Crooke had anticipated would probably bar the village's main street. They sent the collection of farm carts, wooden boxes and bales of hay flying wildly in all directions. The Hitler Youth scattered for safety. There were curses and angry shouts everywhere in German as they tried to get out of the animals' way. Before they could recover, the Destroyers had followed, spraying the street on both sides. The youths dropped in their tracks, caught completely off guard. Then they broke completely, fleeing from the hail of fire. Throwing away their weapons, the survivors hurled themselves through the nearest doorways.

The panic-stricken Hitler Youth were easy meat for the hardened veterans. Giving them no time to recover, the Destroyers poured burst after burst through the open doorways and shattered windows on both sides as they ran, leaving a score of screaming, dying children behind them.

Then the mayhem and murder was over. They were out of the village and running to the thick pine woods beyond, panting for the cover of the trees.

Behind them the crackle of small arms grew fainter and fainter and finally died away altogether. Exhausted, they crawled into a deep thicket of pines, moving in backwards and closing the undergrowth behind them, and flung themselves down on the needle-covered ground.

Crooke, crouching on guard, overlooking the road that led from the village, gave them five minutes to recover, while he eyed the road anxiously in case they were being followed. Finally he turned to Thaelmann. 'All right, Thaelmann, break out the gear.'

Wiping the sweat off his brow, the German unslung the *Wehrmacht* rucksack off his shoulders. He untied the lacings with fingers that still trembled slightly and brought out the documents. 'Colonel Koch had these specially prepared for us,' he said. 'The document is genuine, it's just the details which are fake.' He handed each Destroyer one of the green documents. *'Fremdarbeiterausweis,'* he explained, 'a foreign worker's pass.'

'Yes, we had to find a difficult nationality for us,' Crooke explained. 'There are plenty of Germans who could trip us up if we pretended to be French or – say – Russian. So Colonel Koch and Commander Mallory picked a tough language and nationality for us.' He forced a smile. 'So the lot of you are now honorary Latvians.'

'Something I've always wanted to be,' Stevens said, staring at the pass.

'Remember, if there's any talking to be done, leave it to me,' Thaelmann warned in his serious German way. 'The rest of you stick to *"nix versteh"*. Then show your pass.'

Stevens looked up from admiring his photograph. 'I'm really a pretty handsome bloke when you come to think about it, aren't I? No wonder the bints is crazy about me. It's me profile,' he simpered, holding his dirty fingers delicately under his unshaven chin. 'Regular John Barrymore I am!'

Crooke laughed. 'All right, let's get on with it. Thaelmann, label them, will you?'

He reached in his rucksack again and brought out a small tin of white paint and a brush, then a plastic stencil. 'O-S-T,' he read the letters out. *'Ost* mean "East" in German. The Nazis label all their foreign labour from the eastern countries with it for easy identification.'

The Yank shook his head in disbelief. 'Christ on a crutch, wouldya believe it?' he exclaimed. 'Like goddam steers! It's the first time I've ever been branded.' But he submitted to having the letters stencilled on the small of his jacket back like the rest of them. When Thaelmann was finished, Stevens did the same for him, then threw the stencil deep into the pines.

Crooke examined Thaelmann's work and nodded. 'Looks okay to me. So this is the situation,' he continued. 'We're Latvians, who have been working in the Lorenz electrical factory in Berlin. The factory has been bombed out and we've been ordered to make our way to the Lorenz factory in Munich. We've not got any travel authorization. Koch couldn't provide that. But apparently there are hundreds of thousands of foreign workers roaming around Germany without proper authority, and in the last resort we've got these.' He rummaged in the rucksack and brought out what looked like a handful of fountain pens. 'The latest SOE device,' he explained. 'A genuine German fountain pen, a popular cheap model called a *Tintenkuli*, but the SOE boffins have done a little bit of modifying. If you press this end here,' he indicated the cap, 'a compressed air cartridge will fire a twenty-two slug which kills at fifteen yards.'

'These and our knives,' Crooke added, as he gave each man two of the cheap pens, 'are all we've got in the way of weapons. But they'll arouse no suspicion if we're stopped and searched. Okay?'

They nodded.

'All right, Gippo, collect up the machine pistols and dump them in the bushes and then let's be getting out of–' Crooke stopped suddenly and swung round as youthful voices echoed up from the road. 'Quick, duck!'

The Destroyers threw themselves flat and, parting the undergrowth, peered cautiously at the procession of black-clad youths straggling up the dusty farm road.

They were the boys who had defended the village. Now they were retreating after their ambush, carrying as much looted ammunition and weapons as possible. Most of them had American carbines and MIs, as well as their own Schmeisser machine pistols, slung over their shoulders; and a couple staggered under the weight of gleaming belts of ammunition and the half-inch machine guns which they had dismantled from the stricken Shermans.

Suddenly Stevens nudged Crooke in the ribs. 'Take a shufti at that, sir,' he whispered. 'Behind that Charlie with the bazooka.' Crooke recognized Cooper. Blood was pouring down the side of his face and he was swaying from side to side, as two tall skinny boys in shorts urged him forward with vicious jabs in the back.

But Cooper was obviously at the end of his strength. His big legs sagged under him and he sank to the ground. For a moment or two the youths kicked him viciously. But their kicks had no effect. Cooper could not or would not get up. A group of boys gathered around the fallen sergeant, obviously discussing what they should do with him, as if he were a latter-day Gulliver and they a mob of Lilliputians.

A fat boy who had lagged behind the rest of the column stopped at the group. Over his shoulder he bore a couple of khaki-coloured blankets and an American poncho. In his hand he carried a jerry can, also obviously looted from the Fourth's vehicles. His arrival was greeted by a chorus of jeers and laughter from the others.

Thaelmann cocked his head to the faint wind to catch their words. 'They're asking him why he didn't bring a tank with him as well,' he reported in a whisper. 'And why the blankets. Was he thinking of having a little shut-eye in the middle of the battle?'

The fat boy was obviously angered by their comments. Petulantly he flung the two blankets over the American lying in the middle of the road. Cooper writhed but could not escape from their soft suffocation.

The boys laughed and talked among themselves, pointing at the fat boy scornfully, but Thaelmann could not make out their words.

But the Destroyers did not need an interpreter to understand what happened next. Suddenly the fat boy flipped open the top of the jerry can, upturned it and began to pour its contents over the blankets.

'*Zuruck!*' the fat boy yelled suddenly at the top of his young voice. The others had not grasped what he intended doing, but the loud command had its effect. They jumped back startled. The next moment the fat boy struck a match on the seat of his pants and flung it at the petrol-soaked blankets.

There was a muffled explosion followed by a sheet of ugly red flame, tinged with black oily flumes. Immediately the blankets began to burn fiercely. Cooper writhed and jerked under them, trying to escape their stifling horror.

Stevens half rose to his feet, but Crooke grabbed him hastily. 'Get down!' he hissed.

'But we've got to help him, sir,' Stevens protested. 'We can't let the poor bastard croak like that!'

'It's too late.'

With one final desperate burst of strength, Cooper had risen to his feet. The blankets dropped from his burning body. Blinded by the flames, his outstretched arms and body blazing fiercely, he staggered forward a few paces. The cries of joy died in the youths' throats. They started back in horror as the flaming monster stamped towards them. Then the big American NCO, now almost consumed by the flames, toppled over the empty jerry can. He fell to the ground, his head lying in a puddle of fire. It was the last thing the Destroyers saw before the jerry can exploded and enveloped the whole road in one long vicious stab of flame.

The youths had gone. In their fear they had abandoned much of their loot. The road was littered with US equipment. But the horrified Destroyers had no eyes for the weapons. Their gaze was fixed on the charred corpse which lay in the middle of the road, and next to it a crude 'W' scratched with a Hitler

Youth dagger.

'You know what that means, don't you?' Crooke asked.

The Destroyers nodded grimly; they knew.

It was the mark of the Werewolf.

## Section Two

## THE ALPINE REDOUBT

'My guess is that Patton is in for a big damn surprise if he thinks that he's gonna walk through the Redoubt like he did Franconia.'

*Major Falk, OSS, to the Destroyers*

# ONE

Thick smoke lay heavy over the shattered city. Before the war its cobbled, medieval streets had echoed to the regimented stamp of Hitler's brown-shirted legions. Then half a million throats, fervent with mass hysteria, had screamed *'Heil Hitler'*, as that coarse Austrian voice had shouted its defiance at the world from a thousand loud-speakers. In those years the bold black, white and red swastika flags had flapped proudly in the breeze and Nuremberg had boasted that it was the 'home of the National Socialist Party'.

But that had been long ago. Ever since January 1945, British and American bombers had pounded the city regularly and now the medieval city lay in ruins. Everywhere were rust-coloured piles of rubble from shattered houses, dotted here and there by twisted lamp standards and steel girders.

In the rain which had begun to fall as the Destroyers shuffled into the old city, Nuremberg presented a scene of sordid horror. Here and there a gutted building still smouldered from the raid of the night before, its stench joining that of the dead buried below the heaps of stone that had once been proud burghers' houses.

They turned a corner. To their right there was a burned-out fire engine, its crew still in position, one behind the other next to the heat-buckled metal ladder, as if they were ready to spring into action at any moment.

Cynically, Stevens raised his cloth cap at the leading fireman. *'Guten Tag,'* he said in an atrocious German accent.

'Knock it off,' the Yank whispered. 'You want the Krauts to get wise to us?' His eyes indicated the crowds ahead around the shattered station.

But as they sauntered closer, their caps

pulled well down over their faces, the Destroyers realized that there was no need to worry. On all sides they could hear the babble of half a dozen languages they could identify – French, Flemish, Russian, Italian, Danish and Polish – and another half dozen they couldn't. It seemed as if half the nationalities in Europe were crowded into the forecourt of Nuremberg's *Hauptbahnhof,* all moving blindly westward, feeling their way by some herd instinct towards the American lines and safety.

'Well, how the hell do we find the OSS guys?' the Yank snarled, as they found a free place by a wall, and stared at the scene. 'Spies don't go around with a lousy great sign on their chests saying what they are,' he added, looking at Crooke.

Crooke shrugged. 'I know, Jones. But Colonel Koch said the OSS chaps had been informed we were coming. They'd be keeping an eye open for us.'

'But why the *Hauptbahnhof?*' Thaelmann objected, lowering his voice as a couple of lordly civilian policemen in their tall leather hats and jackboots strode through the crowd of chattering foreigners, as if they weren't there, automatically expecting that a path would be opened for them.

'It's the only possible place,' Crooke answered. 'Where else can you meet someone in a place like this? Look around you.' He indicated the group of furtive black marketeers in an alcove, haggling over prices and a handful of poilus, obviously paroled prisoners-of-war in their faded blue uniforms and wooden sabots, staring hungrily at a couple of Russian girls in long full skirts and embroidered blouses. 'This is the only remaining centre of activity. This is what I want you to do, Stevens, you and Gippo take the far side of the station. Yank, you and Peters take the other end. Thaelmann and I will cover you, in case there's any trouble.'

'And what are we supposed to do, sir?' Peters asked.

'Good question. Keep a weather eye open for anyone who looks as if he could be an

OSS agent.'

'That's a bit of a tall order, sir.'

'I know. But I have an idea that our man will contact us first, not the other way round.' He tapped his breast pocket as if to check whether the deadly little fountain pen was still there. 'And watch yourselves. No doubt there'll be police spies circulating among the foreign workers.'

The Destroyers nodded and slowly broke away, merging casually into the throng. While they did so, Crooke and Thaelmann positioned themselves near a white arrow pointing downwards, above the legend *Luftschutzbunker* (air-raid shelter) and watched them and their immediate neighbours carefully for any suspicious signs.

Time went by. Suddenly a soft voice next to Crooke asked, *'Haben Sie Feuer?'*

Thaelmann reacted immediately. *'Ja, ich hab' Feuer,'* he answered and turned to look at the man who had asked for a light.

It was a little man in topboots and rusty black suit, who looked as if he had not shaved for the last week or so. He held up his hand-rolled, black tobacco cigarette for the proffered light. *'Danke,'* he said hoarsely and blew out a stream of evil-smelling smoke.

*'Bitte,'* Thaelmann answered coldly. But the little man made no attempt to go away. He studied them with his cold dark eyes, then asked, 'Got anything?'

'Anything – what?' Thaelmann replied, puzzled.

The man sniggered. 'Man, what do you think we're all here for? Come off it.' He grinned knowingly, as if Thaelmann were faking ignorance for reasons known only to himself. 'Coffee, butter, sugar, potatoes?'

'No,' Thaelmann said firmly. 'I've got nothing for the Black Market. *Hau ab* – beat it!'

But the little man was not offended, neither did he move away. He jerked a dirty thumb at Crooke. 'What's up with him?' he asked. 'Why don't he say nothing?'

'Foreign worker,' Thaelmann said shortly. 'Latvian.'

'Latvian, eh?' He grinned and shot a rapid flow of words at the one-eyed officer in a completely unknown tongue, while Crooke stared at him in blank incomprehension.

The black marketeer grinned, but there was no answering light in his eyes. 'You're not a Latvian,' he said. 'I spent ten years in Riga. I know the language. He don't,' he added for Thaelmann's benefit. Crooke felt for the fountain pen. Out of the corner of his eye he saw to his alarm that two German military policemen had appeared at the entrance of the bombed station.

The little man followed the direction of his gaze. 'Don't worry,' he said softly. 'I won't shop you to the "chain dog".'

'Who are you?' Crooke asked in bad German.

The little man did not reply. Instead he crooked his finger at them. 'I'll lead. You – and the others – can follow.'

Crooke hesitated.

The two German MPs, both of whom had machine pistols slung across their chests, were eyeing them suspiciously. One of them said something to his companion. The latter nodded. Slowly they began to stride down the steps, full of the majestic, self-importance of policemen the world over.

That decided Crooke. He flashed a glance at the other Destroyers, and hurried after the little man who had already disappeared into the crowd.

The freight yard behind the station was a mess of smashed, twisted locomotives and shattered coaches. The Allied air forces had obviously done their work well. Nothing had moved in or out of Nuremberg *Hauptbahnhof's* freight yard for weeks. And over all hung a heavy pungent odour which made them gasp for breath, as if they had been struck physically across the face. 'Bloody hell,' Stevens cursed in English, totally forgetting his cover, 'what's that sodding pong?'

The little man, who was a dozen yards in front of them, picking his way over the rusty tracks, turned and said in fluent American English. 'Coffins – a whole goddam train load of 'em!'

He pointed to a line of coaches to their right. 'Filled with rotting dead bodies when a battalion of infantry got caught here in the raid before last as they were in transit. That's what the locals say, and that's the reason nobody ever comes here any more. That's dead flesh you can smell.' He chuckled.

'Say,' the Yank began, 'what kind of a deal are you trying to...'

'Come on,' the little man commanded, cutting him short in the manner of a man who was used to giving orders.

Obediently they followed, holding their noses as they came level with the train from which the smell came. The little man stopped. Carefully he looked to left and right, then indicated the last two coaches. 'Take a peek at them!' They did as he commanded.

At the end of the ghost train, a yellow liquid dripped persistently from the cracks in the two coaches. 'The locals think it's pus from the bodies,' the little man explained.

'But it isn't. Nothing of the sort. Just plain old cabbages – rotting cabbages!'

Crooke strode up to him and grabbed him by the lapels of his shabby jacket. 'All right, what's the damn game?'

But the little man's face showed no fear. His eyes were as calm and as cynical as ever. 'No game, Lieutenant Crooke,' he answered evenly and released himself from Crooke's hold. 'Just the usual OSS tricks.'

'OSS?'

'Sure,' the little man answered. 'We've been expecting you all day. Surely Colonel Koch told you about me and my team?'

'Do you mean...?'

'Naturally. I'm Major Falk!'

# TWO

Falk led them to the last coach of the 'ghost train'. It was surmounted at the end by a strange towerlike affair. 'The Krauts used them for an armed guard in Russia in case the train was attacked by partisans,' he explained. 'You can see the loopholes on either side.'

Crooke nodded coldly. For some reason he had taken an instinctive dislike to Falk. He could not put his finger on it exactly, but there was something about the OSS Major which made him wary. 'I see. But what's that got to do with us, Major Falk?'

'Let me show you.' He clambered nimbly up the iron steps and entered the narrow guard's compartment, while they crowded behind him. He pulled a rusty iron handle and the inner wall slid back. Grinning at their obvious surprise, he extended his right hand, palm outwards. 'Enter, said the spider to the fly. Welcome to our humble home.'

He stepped to one side and revealed a straw-covered floor on which two men were squatting, pistols in their hands. Obviously they had been taken by surprise.

'Sorry fellers,' Falk said easily. 'I know. I forgot to give the signal.' He indicated the Destroyers. 'These are the guys we've been expecting. Okay, come on in and meet my team.'

As they entered, staring at the gloomy interior of the big coach, he pushed back the cunningly concealed entrance door, and said: 'The one with the blond mop – that's Gottwald, he's a Kraut.'

Gottwald, a big, raw-boned ex-POW who had volunteered to work with the OSS, held out his hand in the Continental fashion and they shook it.

'And the fat guy – when we first dropped, I thought he'd need two 'chutes – he's Karel, our radio operator. He's a Free Czech.'

Karel, an unpleasantly fat man, with a week's growth of beard, who looked as if he sweated a lot and didn't wash enough, waved his dimpled pudgy hand and gave them a slight bow. 'Good to meet you,' he said in a guttural accent.

'This is an ideal set-up,' Major Falk explained, as they crouched down on the floor and looked around curiously at the ancient potbellied stove in one corner and the powerful new radio transmitter in the other, on which rested a flickering candle. 'Nobody comes around here now because of the bodies,' he chuckled, 'and we're right in the centre of things. No risk of the usual hotel-room checks the Krauts run periodically. And we wheel and deal to keep body and soul alive.' He indicated the stack of Lucky Strike cartons near the radio. 'We kid the guys on the black market that they're hot because we've looted them from Red Cross parcels intended for American POWs. That way there are no questions asked.'

'Must be a pretty strange sort of life,

Major,' the Yank said. 'You guys play it near the knuckle, I guess.'

Falk nodded. 'Sure, it's kinda rugged at times, but so far we've survived. After all, you know, there are about ten million Krauts and foreign workers on the move in the Reich these days – refugees from the East, bugging out from the Russians, deserters, Kraut soldiers who've lost their units in the general ballsup. The cops can't check everybody. And we're' – he indicated his companions, who sat there in silence – 'just three guys in the whole sorry mess.' He paused and stared at the Destroyers keenly. 'But then I don't need to tell you fellers that, you've seen it all. What are your orders, Lieutenant Crooke, and how can I help you?'

'You've heard of the Alpine Redoubt?' Crooke said.

'Sure, we've been keeping our eyes open for traffic heading that way, haven't we, Karel?'

The fat Czech grunted. Like Gottwald, Crooke noted, he was strangely tense, in spite of his silence.

'In the last seven or eight days we've counted ten convoys heading that way. Mostly SS, but there was one full of ex-submarine personnel from the *Kriegsmarine,* who've got no boats left. Fanatics the lot of them,' Falk concluded. 'They'll hold the line when the ordinary German *Landser* is heading back home.'

'The Redoubt is a serious proposition then?' Crooke asked.

'Serious! Sure it's serious. My guess is that Patton is in for a big damn surprise if he thinks that he's gonna walk through the Redoubt like he did Franconia.'

'That Patton's a tough baby, Major,' the Yank commented.

Falk shrugged. 'Between you and me, soldier, I can take General Patton – and *leave* him. I served with him at the beginning in Africa when he commanded the old Second Corps and I kinda grew to dislike the things he represented, if you know what I mean?'

'No I don't,' Crooke said coldly.

Falk did not seem to hear. 'Okay, Crooke,' he continued brightly. 'Now what's the deal?'

'We want to get into the Redoubt,' Crooke said. 'What would you suggest as a route?'

'The position's pretty fluid at the moment. I think you'd have a pretty good chance of slipping through before the Kraut resistance hardens. I'd suggest you swing south-east of Nuremberg and head for Munich. But avoid the railroads and the autobahn – they're too well guarded. I'd skip Munich itself too. You could get screwed there pretty easily. There are a lot of Kraut deserters there and the place is swarming with cops. From there I'd head due south, crossing the Austrian border somewhere between Bad Reichenhall and Schwarzbach. I've heard there's not much activity round about there. And there are plenty of places to hide out. I know because I was down there on a skiing vacation in the thirties when I was a student at Munich.' He hesitated a moment, his dark eyes looking at the straw-covered floor, as if he did not want Crooke to see the look in them. 'But if you could give me a few more exact details, perhaps I could help you better. What exactly is your mission in the Redoubt? You see,' he went on hastily, 'it covers a helluva big area and it's pretty rugged terrain, if you don't know it.'

'We are to locate the Werewolf head-quarters,' Crooke said slowly, his distrust of the strange little OSS Major growing by the minute. 'We've got a special assignment to carry out there.'

Falk whistled softly. 'The Hawk's HQ! Wow, that's some assignment!'

Over his shoulder, Crooke caught the quick change of expression on the fat Czech's face.

'You've heard of the Hawk, then?' Crooke asked.

'Sure, he's some tough baby. He's a guy I wouldn't like to tackle from what I've heard of his reputation.' He lifted his eyes and stared directly at the British officer. 'Why are you guys gonna risk tangling with him?'

'Hell, we're big boys; we ain't scared of no Hawk,' the Yank snarled before Crooke could stop him. 'We're here to kill the Kraut bastard!'

'*Kill him!*' Falk blurted out.

Karel's fat mouth dropped open stupidly. He muttered something in a language that Crooke could not understand.

Falk pulled himself together quickly. 'Boy, rather you guys than me! Okay, you're going to need transportation, if you can't use the railroads or main roads. What about push cycles? Can all you guys ride a bike?' The Destroyers nodded.

'Good. Well, I suggest that we try to organize you fellers some bikes on the black market. It won't be easy, but we've got the goodies that the Krauts are real crazy for. Karel, you grab the Luckies and Gottwald break out the bean coffee.'

The big German dragged a small sack from their store. He slit open the end and started to pour the beans into small brown paper packets. 'One hundred grams in each packet,' Falk explained. 'It'd be too noticeable if we tried to flog the whole shoot up at the station.

118

Hell, that sack's worth near on three thousand Reichsmarks on the black market. You could get yourself a nice hole in the head in some dark back alley for that kind of dough in Germany these days. Those black market boys play rough, especially the Polacks.' He turned to the two OSS agents. 'Better check your weapons,' he ordered.

Obediently they checked their Walther Police Specials. Then they thrust them back into their waistbands again and picked up their various packages.

'Okay, Crooke,' Falk said, 'we'll get on the stick and see if we can rustle up those pushbikes pronto.' He paused at the door and rapped on it three times with his middle knuckle. 'When you hear that, with a one-second interval between each knock, you'll know it's safe to open. It'll be us.'

'Are you going with the other two?' Crooke asked.

'Yeah, we've got to move fast if we're going to get your gear before midnight. Much as I like you guys' company, I'd like you to take a powder before dawn. You understand, don't you?' He flashed Crooke what he obviously thought was a winning smile, but there was no real warmth in it.

'Yes,' Crooke answered.

'If I were you, I'd get some sacktime. It's gonna be a rough night and I guess you've had a rugged day behind you. You don't need to worry about posting sentries, none of the local Krauts would dare come up here after dark, believe you me.'

Falk swung a long intense look around the dark interior of his hideout, almost as if he wanted to impress its details on his mind for some reason known only to himself, then he opened the door and passed through. The others followed. 'Be seeing you guys,' he said from outside, as Stevens closed the door. 'Bye.'

For a moment the Destroyers crouched in silence in the dark flickering interior. The Yank yawned loudly and stretched himself out in the dirty straw. 'Boy, that feels good,' he sighed, closing his eyes. 'Better than a feather bed back home.'

Crooke could see his men were beat. They had had no sleep for over twenty-four hours and the ambush had taken it out of them. Even a couple of hours' rest before they set off would be better than nothing. 'All right,' he said wearily, 'Gippo, you can take first stag.'

'The Major said we didn't need to post sentries, sir,' Peters objected mildly.

'That's what the Major said,' Crooke answered without rancour. 'I think different.'

Obediently Gippo opened the door and crept outside into the little dark tower. 'Okay?' Crooke called up to him on his perch. It was completely black in the freight yard now. The Germans were observing a total blackout. Nuremberg had been too badly bombed over these last few months for them to take any chances.

'Yessir,' Gippo whispered, as if the yard were full of enemy soldiers. Like all Egyptians, Gippo did not like being alone in the dark.

Crooke grinned to himself. 'Okay, Gippo, give me a shout in an hour's time, I'll take over the stag then.'

Within seconds of his head touching his rolled-up jacket, which served him as a pillow, Crooke was fast asleep.

# THREE

The SS came three hours later.

Like grey wolves they slunk across the abandoned freight yard, squirming under the coaches, flitting silently from train to train, coming ever closer to the 'ghost train'. A young trooper hit his helmet against the metal coupling, and gave an angry curse, which was stifled a moment later by the NCO's urgent whisper.

But the sound sufficed to alert the bone-tired Destroyers, drugged with sleep, as it reached down into that part of their being which never slept.

Hastily Crooke scrambled to his feet. It seemed that he had hardly closed his eyes since Stevens had relieved him on guard, but a quick glance at his watch told him that had been nearly an hour ago. Around him everything was hectic yet controlled activity as the Destroyers rose out of the straw, grabbing their pathetic little weapons, sensing as he had done that the alien sound outside boded no good for them. 'Put that candle out,' he whispered.

Peters clapped his hand round it and blew it out, just as Stevens opened the door and hissed, 'Jerries, sir. The yard's full of them!'

'Come on. Everybody outside,' Crooke ordered in a low voice. 'Sharpish, and for Christ's sake, no noise!'

Hastily they squeezed through the door and took up their positions in the tower, peering through the loopholes into the darkness.

'The bastards are up in the next line of freight cars,' the Yank whispered.

'And they're behind us as well, sir,' Peters reported.

Gippo drew his knife and clicked back the switch. Five inches of steel shot out noiselessly. 'This is being better, yes,' he said softly.

Crooke nodded to himself, proud of his men's reaction. In spite of their attitude back in London, he knew they'd fight. There wasn't a coward among them. But already he had spotted a dozen of the stealthy shadows outside, all obviously well-armed, and he knew even the Destroyers' undoubted bravery and determination would be no use against submachine guns.

'Do you think they're looking for us?' Stevens asked, not taking his eyes off the dark shapes.

'Of course. Why else all the fuss? If they were looking for deserters or black marketeers or what have you, they wouldn't be advancing in battle formation. They know we're here and they know we're armed. They're taking no chances.'

'Yeah, what kinda goddam chance have we got with them electric peashooters,' the Yank complained bitterly. 'But, say, how did the Krauts know we're here?'

'I don't know,' Crooke hissed. 'And I'm damned if I'm going to wait here and find out. We're making tracks now.'

'But how, sir?' Stevens asked. 'They'll have

thrown a cordon round the whole place if they know we're here. You know what the Jerries are like – thorough bastards!'

Crooke jerked a finger upwards. 'Over the roof. Quick. Off with your boots and pull your socks over them. We've got to be as quiet as possible.'

Hastily they did as he ordered. One by one they squirmed up the little iron ladder on to the roof, crawling over its top on their stomachs to keep their silhouettes as low as possible.

Below, the SS were only a dozen feet away now. As he squirmed along the damp slippery roof on his belly, Crooke caught a momentary glimpse of the silver SS rune reflecting some light or other. But he had no time to inform the others. In a moment the Germans would be trying to get into the coach they had just left and by that time they would have to be well away.

The first roof proved easy to cross, in spite of its awkward downward curve; then they were able to support themselves by hanging

126

on to the metal ventilation sheathing which ran its whole length. But when Crooke reached out in the darkness to find a grip on the next coach, he found to his alarm that the sheathing was absent. Urgently he craned his head round and whispered to the waiting Destroyers, 'Gippo, you're the lightest. I'm going to stretch out between the two coaches, you try to crawl over me. And for God's sake make it quick!'

Gingerly Crooke reached out till his whole body was extended between the two coaches. He gripped the opposite edge and whispered, 'Okay.' The next instant he felt Gippo's weight descend on his legs. 'Now sir?' 'Yes,' Crooke said through gritted teeth, as he took the strain. Gippo was a lightweight, but at that moment he seemed to weigh a ton. Crooke tightened his leg muscles. Desperately his stiffened outstretched fingers dug into the wood on the other coach like talons. The half-breed was almost to the other side now. He could feel his heart beating furiously. Suddenly one of Crooke's nails snapped off. He bit his teeth together to stifle the pain. Gippo crawled on: he'd nearly done. Another nail went and an agonizing pain shot through his hand. Grimly he dug his teeth into his bottom lip. And then the strain was gone and Gippo was gripping both his wrists and trying to pull him to the other side. For a moment he hung there like a bridge, unable to move. Behind him at the far end of the coach he could hear the SS clambering up the ladder of the watchtower as they tried to find the entrance to the OSS hideout. With a last effort, Crooke forced his muscles to work. Gippo gave a heave and he was across, his hands trembling violently with the strain.

'Come on, you next Stevens.' Together, he and Gippo extended their hands until their fingers touched those of the little cockney. Soon Stevens was across the gap and he could help Gippo to get the rest across, while Crooke knelt there, sucking his wounded hand.

A couple of minutes later they dropped

softly to the ground between the lines. Behind them the SS were hammering on the door of the coach. Someone shouted. *'Los – aufmachen!* Open up or we'll fire!'

Up ahead two dark shapes, rifles slung over their shoulders, were leaning against a shattered locomotive, hands cupped around the red tips of their glowing cigarettes. Crooke assessed the situation quickly. The only way they could get out of the yard was past the two sentries. 'Okay, get them,' he commanded. 'But for God's sake keep it quiet!'

Behind them the sound of the hammering grew louder.

In their stockinged feet the Yank and Peters disappeared round the other side of the line of shattered coaches. As softly as cats, they came up behind the unsuspecting sentries whose attention was occupied by the events at the other end of the 'ghost train'.

Suddenly the taller of the two swung round in alarm, fumbling for his rifle. But he was too late. Before he could shout, the Yank had grabbed the back of his coal-scuttle helmet and pulled it down. The chin strap slipped under the German's adam's apple and stifled his cry. Peters did the same for the other. Panting with the effort, the Yank released his hold and let the man slump to the ground. At his side, the smooth-cheeked boy whom Peters held tightly in his grip stared at his dead companion in horror, his eyes bulging wildly.

The rest of the Destroyers hurried over to them, clinging to the shadows. Thaelmann thrust his unshaven face close to the boy's. 'How did you know we were here?' he asked in German.

The boy gasped for breath and indicated that Peters should loosen his hold a little.

He did so and the boy gasped for air. 'I don't know,' he said bravely, but his eyes were full of fear.

Thaelmann grabbed him by the neck and squeezed hard. *'The truth!'* he demanded.

At the rear of the 'ghost train', the Germans were shouting at each other angrily. Obviously they had discovered that the birds had flown. Crooke tightened his grip on his fountain pen. In a few seconds the Boche would come running.

The youth's panic-filled eyes conceded defeat. 'I'll speak,' he panted.

Thaelmann relaxed his grip.

'We were ordered … from the barracks,' the words came in gasps as he fought for air. 'Someone telephoned … I don't know who… The Sergeant said … spies, Ami spies.'

Crooke gave Peters a barely perceptible nod. The latter's fingers sought for the soft spots behind the young SS man's ears. With a grunt he exerted pressure. The German stiffened. His back arched. Convulsively he shuddered. A second later a terrible choking noise came from deep down within his throat. There was the sound of something snapping. His helmeted head lolled on to his shoulders.

'Come on,' Crooke hissed, as the cries of rage rose in volume behind them, *let's go!*'

Peters let the young SS man slump to the gravel. Heavily-booted feet came stamping their way. In the old city the air-raid sirens began to sound their chill warning of impending doom. The Destroyers turned and began to run.

The motors died away in the distance. The great four-engined Lancasters had gone for good. Far away to the west of the city, the first of the air-raid sirens sounded the all clear. One after another other sirens took up the call, getting ever closer to where the Destroyers crouched in the rubble.

They rubbed the brick dust from their faces and licked their parched lips. The air was heavy with the smell of burning wood and brick dust. Behind them street after street was blocked with debris where shattered apartment houses had cascaded into them. The debris was covered with tangles of fallen wires and the snakes of the hoses with which the harassed firemen were trying to put out the hundreds of fires. But the flames were too powerful for the handful of firemen.

Stevens poked his head up and surveyed

the scene of confusion, with shouting civilians and a handful of officials running back and forth, trying to rescue a few pathetic possessions, scraping out the buried victims, bellowing useless orders. 'Sodding hell,' he gasped, 'yer could almost feel sorry for the Jerries after that lot!'

'Feel sorry for yourself,' Crooke snapped. 'We're in a fix – a bad fix.'

'Them bombers did us a good turn, sir,' Peters said and wiped his dirty, dust-covered face. 'I'll never say another bad word against them blue jobs. They kept the SS off our backs – that's for sure.'

'Yeah, the heat's off for a while,' the Yank agreed. 'But what I can't figure out is how them jerks got on to us. Who gave them the tip-off?'

'Get yer finger out, mate,' Stevens said scornfully. 'Yer must be sodding wet behind the ears. Yer don't need no crystal ball to see who shopped us! It's as obvious as the nose on yer mug. Them Yanks from the OSS gave the Jerries the wire!'

'You are right,' Gippo said. He turned to the others. 'They have betrayed us. They are bad men, it is speaking to reason, yes.'

'Yes,' Stevens said, leaving his fractured English uncorrected for once. 'And them Werewolf blokes was waiting for us when we went up with the Fourth Armoured too. They knew we was coming. If you ask me, sir,' he addressed himself to Crooke, 'I'd say we've been shopped ever since we left General Patton's headquarters. Some sod's got us by the short and curlies and won't let go.'

Crooke gave a little shrug and tore his mind away from the almost unbelievable thought that an ally – an American to boot – would betray them to the enemy. 'We'll do what the Destroyers have always done in tricky situations like this – we'll go forward.'

'Just what I thought we'd bloody well do,' Stevens said with mock dourness. 'Situation normal – the Destroyers right up the creek, without a sodding paddle among the lot of them!'

# FOUR

They were following the tramlines through a quiet little Bavarian country town. It was an old ploy for getting through an unknown city in the early morning without asking questions. Follow the most crowded tram and it will usually take you to the station. Once there, follow the most crowded tram from the other direction and if you are lucky it will take you into the suburbs.

Another shabby, blue-painted number four tram rattled by, with sleepy workmen hanging from its side. It was 'their' tram. They plodded on after it.

A few minutes later they halted a hundred yards from the busy *Bahnhof* and surveyed the crowds, trying to assess which of the trams were taking the most people eastwards. They decided on the number fourteen.

They set off again over a small bridge, decorated with the rampant lion of Bavaria. Beyond, the jagged gables of the medieval houses were starkly silhouetted against the clear morning sky. The further east they went, the clearer the sky became. There was a hint of snow in the air.

They entered the suburbs: pompous, red-brick villas, built at the turn of the century, now a little shabby and decayed after nearly six years of war. Abandoning the tramline, in case there might be a checkpoint on the main road as it left town, they turned into a tree-lined avenue, running parallel. From either side came the morning sounds of people waking up and making breakfast – the faint cries of children, the rattle of spoons, the rusty squeak of someone opening a garage door that hadn't been oiled for a long time. And everywhere there was the warm tempting smell of *ersatz* coffee.

Crooke looked at his men. He knew they'd have to take a break soon and get some food. They hadn't eaten for over forty-eight hours. Besides their appearance was getting suspicious. They needed a wash and shave, with the tiny SOE-issue safety razors they all carried.

A large white-stucco house loomed up in front of them, set back from the avenue in a small park, its drive fringed by thick pines. 'Hold it, lads,' he ordered softly.

Gratefully they leaned against a wooden fence and stared apathetically into nothing. Crooke saw that they were at the end of their tether.

For a moment or two, he stared at the house thoughtfully, noting that the windows on the ground floor were shuttered and bared and that every window upstairs was closed. Nor was there any smoke curling from the chimneys as was the case in the other houses. Either its inhabitants were long sleepers, he told himself, or the house was empty.

'Stevens, Gippo.'

The two ex-lags stumbled over to him. 'Sir?'

'See that place?'

They nodded.

'What are our chances of breaking into it without too much fuss and bother?'

Gippo's eyes sparkled. Crooke had appealed to his professional pride and the challenge made him forget his weariness. 'For me, I am saying it is a piece of biscuit.'

'*Cake*,' Stevens corrected him. He sucked his teeth thoughtfully. 'If no one's living in the sod, sir – and it looks pretty much like that – we could be in in a couple of minutes.'

'All right, you two,' Crooke said, 'we'll break in. What do we have to do?'

'See that ladder and bucket leaning against that tree?'

Crooke turned and looked at the ladder, which someone had probably left out the night before by mistake. 'Yes.'

'Two of the lads can grab that – casual like. Somebody else can take the bucket. We walk in as if we've come to do a job, in case any of the neighbours are watching. Then leave the rest to me and Gippo.'

Two minutes later they were round the back of the house, hidden from view on all sides by the tall pines. Stevens nodded to Gippo. The half-breed picked up a stone and flung it hard and accurately against the side of the house. The sound echoed upwards and died away. Scanning the house anxiously, Stevens waited for a cry or a footstep. There was none.

'All right, Gippo,' he whispered.

Together they stole across the wet lawn and tip-toed softly over the leaf-covered gravel path. Swiftly Stevens took a piece of hard plastic out of his pocket and inserted it underneath the lock. While Gippo caught hold of the handle and pulled it hard, Stevens heaved once. The door swung open and Stevens turned, raising his thumb in triumph. 'We're quids in, sir,' he said softly. 'The place is empty.'

Cautiously they entered a big kitchen which smelt of stale cooking and sour milk. While the Yank stood guard by the door Gippo and Stevens began to ransack the cupboards. Slowly but surely a small heap of food began to grow in the centre of the kitchen table: half a salami, its end going green with mould, a complete packet of *Zwieback,* the German rusks, a few slices of black pumpernickel bread wrapped in silver paper, a handful of big onions already beginning to sprout shoots, an end of Tilsiter cheese, a couple of cans of tinned milk. 'Lovely grub,' Stevens said enthusiastically, as the pile grew larger. 'Just what the sodding doctor ordered, what sir?'

Crooke, slumped on a rickety carved chair, grinned wearily. 'You're right there, Stevens – just what the sodding doctor ordered!'

Five minutes later they were wolfing down the strange mixture of bits and pieces while Crooke stood guard at the kitchen door. Satisfied, the Destroyers wandered carefully through the rest of the darkened house. The place was in utter confusion, as if it had been left in a hurry. In the study the doors of the bookcase were open and half a dozen books had been pulled out and left on the floor.

Curiously Thaelmann picked one up and read the title aloud: *'Blood and Honour is my Oath – the History of the Armed SS.'* He dropped it contemptuously, and indicated the somewhat flashy portrait of an SS officer on the wall, said: 'Nazis. Must have fled when they thought the Americans might break through last week.'

Crooke nodded but said nothing. After the food, all he wanted to do was to lie down and sleep. Even the hard polished wooden floor looked inviting. He yawned.

'Boozy Nazis anyhow,' Stevens said behind them. 'Look at them dead soldiers, will yer?' He pointed to the long line of empty bottles along the far wall. *'Korn* – that's gin, isn't it? *Kognak* and *Enzian* – what's that mean in a civilized lingo, Thaelmann?'

But Thaelmann did not have to answer the cockney's question. Another voice did it for him, a female voice. 'It is a local drink,' it said softly. 'Not bad if there is nothing else.'

They spun round. A tall blonde girl stood there, swaying slightly, clad in a sheer silk nightdress that reached to the floor and through which the morning sun shone, outlining her naked body. In one hand she held an empty champagne glass. Impatiently she used it to push back a lock of unruly hair which had fallen down over her blurred but intelligent eyes. She did not move the other hand, for it was clenched round a small gleaming silver pistol: a lady's weapon, but all the same, at that distance, one which would kill very effectively.

'Dead soldiers,' she said almost conversationally in virtually accentless English. 'Funny. We use the same expression.'

Thaelmann recovered first. 'Who are you?' he said, and then, 'Put that pistol down!' He moved forward a step, as if he were about to wrest it from her hand.

She jerked it up threateningly. In spite of the fact that she was obviously drunk, the girl was alert enough. 'Stay there,' she cried in German and then switched back to English again. 'I know how to use this.' She laughed harshly. 'He taught me that well enough.' She indicated the portrait of the black-clad SS officer. 'And a lot of other things too.'

Crooke, his mouth open a little stupidly, stared at the girl.

'Oh yes,' she repeated, 'a lot of things. Pretty ones – and ones which were not so pretty.' She shivered, as if in recollection of some past sexual experience, and her body rippled beneath the silk. In spite of the obvious danger of their position, Gippo's little black eyes devoured the woman's body greedily.

'We're escaped British prisoners-of-war,' Crooke said calmly. 'We broke in because we were hungry.' Cautiously his hand slid down to the pocket containing the SOE pen.

'*Don't move!*' she ordered, 'or I'll shoot.' She let the empty champagne glass drop to the floor, as if to emphasize her threat.

Crooke's hand froze where it was; he could see she wasn't joking. 'Escaped British prisoners-of-war, eh.' She laughed hollowly. 'And he–' she indicated Thaelmann with the pistol '–he speaks fluent German and you are all in civilian clothes. No, my fine Tommies, you are not soldiers. You are spies – miserable little British spies.'

Stevens licked his lips. He knew he had a way with women. Ever since his first experience at the age of eleven with the wife of a neighbour, who had been twice as old, he had never had any difficulty in getting a 'piece of the other', as he called it.

'Miss, you're right.'

Crooke shot him a warning look. But Stevens pretended not to notice. 'But we was forced to do it. We didn't want to come here. You see back in England, they threatened to put our people in the nick if we didn't co-operate. We're just ordinary honest soldiers, who want to survive.' His voice softened winningly, as the blonde listened to his 'spiel'. 'We don't want to die, miss. There's

144

other things yer can do than kill people, ain't there.' Carefully he took one step forward, confident now that he was breaking down her resistance. 'I mean a beautiful young lady like you doesn't want to get herself involved with the police. I can see yer like yer parties – a few drinks, a bit of music, perhaps a bit of the old light fantastic–'

Stevens babbled on and the girl listened, as if mesmerized, to the flood of words. Slowly he took another step forward. And another, never taking his eyes off her plump smooth face, nor ceasing to speak for a moment.

'You know how it is,' Stevens went on. 'A bloke and a girl gets together and they have a bit of fun. I mean what's life for otherwise? Not just to work. All work and no play makes Jack a dull boy, eh?' His dirty hand was perhaps a yard away from the pistol. She didn't seem to notice. Her whole attention was devoted to this strange little man, who talked at high speed and so confidently about things which she only half comprehended.

'Yer only young once and I think you've got to enjoy yourself while you can. I mean, I bet a beautiful young lady like yourself wouldn't say no to a bit of slap and tickle, if it were done the right way.'

His groping fingers were almost touching her now. If she fired, the whole neighbourhood would be alarmed within seconds. In the morning stillness, even the report of that silly little pistol would carry a long way and within seconds the neighbours would come running.

'Now, I'd like to suggest something to you, miss,' Stevens said. 'If you don't say nothing, I won't. I mean you and me could make beautiful music together. I know that.' His thick dirty fingernails caressed the tips of hers as she stood there, her shapely legs thrust apart and silhouetted tightly against the pale green silk. One more second, and Stevens would have the pistol. He could see how the whiteness of her knuckles was beginning to vanish, as she relaxed her hold on it.

'If you'd sort of let go of that...'

Then she squeezed the trigger.

At such close range, the bullet flung Stevens back a clear three feet. He hit the wall behind him hard and slumped down on to the floor. A jet of blood spurted from his shattered shoulder. *'You bitch – you rotten bitch!'* he roared.

The next instant Gippo launched himself forward. He caught the girl in the stomach. She crashed to the floor with the enraged half-breed on top of her. Desperately she squirmed back and forth, her nightgown thrown back to her thighs, as Gippo sought and found her throat.

Muttering incoherently to himself in Arabic, mad with rage at the injury done to his friend, he exerted full pressure on her soft neck. Her eyes bulged and the tongue shot out of her mouth. Frantically her long nails ripped down the side of his face. Gippo did not seem to notice the pain, nor Peters' blow on the back of his head and his cries of warning. Blindly, seeing only her purple face and popping eyes, he crushed the breath and then the life out of her until her wildly contorting body gave one final twitch and was still for good.

When the elderly, jack-booted *Schupos* came crashing into the house, pistols at the ready, he was still slumped over her dead body.

# FIVE

The sergeant in charge of the local police was a huge man with a fat pink neck and a waxed 'Kaiser Bill' moustache which clearly marked him as a World War One *Unteroffizier.* Helped by the other shocked and elderly pot-bellied policemen, whose bemedalled chests bore testimony to their service in the same war, he bundled the Destroyers into a big dank cell, while two other *Schupos* supported Stevens upstairs where he could wait *'fur den Herrn Doktor.'*

From the look on the sergeant's face it was obvious that he had never been confronted with anything quite like this before. He shouted at the downcast prisoners and threatened them with his big pistol a couple of times when they were too slow for him, but his body search was half-hearted and careless. Still shocked by the sight of the half-naked body of the mistress of SS General Dietz, who had been killed in Russia the previous year, he even forgot to remove their belts and bootlaces before he closed the door of the evil-smelling cell on them.

The morning dragged on in heavy silence, broken only by the muted chug-chug of the odd wood-burning farm truck and the periodic rattle when the guard pulled back the bolt of the Judas Hole to stare in at them. For a while the Destroyers had little to say to each other. They were exhausted and utterly depressed by their sudden capture, and Crooke knew they were worried about Stevens; he had been bleeding pretty badly when the German policemen carried him upstairs. Half-heartedly he examined their gloomy cell, which looked as if it had been constructed in the Middle Ages and not lost a single prisoner by escape in all the centuries that had passed since then. The dripping, green-encrusted walls were several feet thick and as far as he could judge made of solid pieces of natural rock. The one window was too small to allow even Gippo to squeeze through and was well out of their reach. As for the door, it was made of rusty iron, several inches thick. It looked as if it would need a charge of dynamite to get it open.

Discouraged, Crooke sank into an uneasy sleep on the cold, hard floor, to be woken by the rattle of the Judas Hole and the police sergeant's bellow. *'Aufstehen – Essen! Dalli – Dalli!* If you want your food, Tommies, open the slot at the bottom of the door – and be sharp about it!'

Gippo opened it and dragged in the canteen of dark potato soup. A heaped plate of sandwiches followed: cheese paste spread over black bread from which protruded what looked like pieces of straw.

The Destroyers champed at the food, taking it in turns to use the one blunt aluminium spoon to eat the lukewarm but spicy soup. While they ate, Crooke consoled himself with the thought that the old police sergeant obviously thought they really were escaped POWs. Why else would he have called them 'Tommies' like that? But what would happen when the more sophisticated police came down from the city to collect them? The Munich people certainly wouldn't buy their story of having broken into the house to find food in the course of an escape from some local stalag. They'd want to see the Red Cross identity card that every POW carried and they'd demand to know the camp from which they had escaped. They'd soon find out that the story which the Destroyers had told the local force was one big lie from beginning to end. And then what?

The afternoon dragged on leadenly. Although they could see that the sun was shining outside, its rays did not penetrate into the cell, and time and time again they found themselves shivering uncontrollably.

At six they heard the sound of heavy, booted feet down the corridor. At first Crooke thought it might be the Munich police coming to fetch them. But it turned out to be the sergeant accompanied by two of his men, pistols drawn as they opened the rusty cell door. He commanded *'Raus – waschen!'* but there was no malice in the sergeant's voice. Crooke even had the impression he sympathized with the prisoners and felt they had got themselves into this mess through no fault of their own: obviously he had not liked the dead woman. During the initial interrogation he had made the continental gesture of lifting a glass to his subordinates and they had nodded sagely, as if that fact explained everything.

Under his watchful supervision they were allowed to wash at the cold water tap and use the latrine. Crooke summoned up his best German and asked: *'Wo ist der Andere?'*

'He's being treated,' the policeman answered gruffly. 'He's all right.'

'Thank you,' Crooke said with relief, 'but where is he?'

'You don't need to know. Here, take your supper.' He handed Crooke a big slice of dark bread spread with a thick bitter substance, which Thaelmann told him later was treacle made from sugarbeet. 'And get that piss bucket inside with you for the night. I'm not having my lads trotting you lot off to the latrines at all hours.'

Locked in their cell, the Destroyers, feeling better now that they had had a good wash, spent the night hours discussing plans of escape, feigning sleep every time one of the guards glanced through the Judas Hole.

With no tools, they realized that it would be impossible to break out. Crooke said, 'It'll only be a matter of hours now before they come to collect us. Allowing for the chaotic transport situation, we won't spend another night in this place, believe you me.'

Thaelmann came up with the best idea. 'In Dachau when I was there, you went to the latrines when you couldn't go on,' he said slowly. 'If you were sick of the whole bloody business and couldn't wait for the ovens,' he went on, making the circulatory motion of rising smoke to indicate the camp crematorium, 'you broke off a sliver of enamel from the inside of the latrine bucket and slit your wrists with it. If you could hide yourself long enough underneath your blanket after evening rollcall, you were dead by morning.' He laughed grimly at the memory. 'Some of the poor bastards worked for days chipping off a piece of enamel of the right size.' He shrugged. 'Perhaps they were trying to put off the evil day, hoping that some noble prince on a white horse would come and rescue them on the next morning. But he never did. It would be the same old five o'clock *Appell* and the same black bastards with their whips.' He broke off suddenly and stared at the dirty stone-flagged floor.

Crooke got up and looked into the evil-smelling bucket, which had once been white but which was now badly discoloured after generations of use by the local drunks and wandering tramps. 'What do you suggest then?'

'Make a knife and then in the morning when they open the door to let us go to the latrines, stab the guard and then,' Thaelmann shrugged a little helplessly, 'well, we'll see.'

'You mean play it by ear,' the Yank said. 'It's the only way out, I guess.'

Crooke nodded. 'It's better than nothing,' he agreed. 'And time's running out for us. Come on, let's get down to it.'

They spent the remaining hours until dawn breaking off a five-inch sliver of enamel, which the Yank embedded in chewing gum – the police sergeant had allowed him to keep it when he had remarked he was an American, for Amis always chewed *Kaugummi*, everyone knew that. Then they wrapped a handkerchief round the chewing gum to form a rough-and-ready handle. 'It's no goddam combat knife,' the Yank commented as he picked up the finished product and tested the edge with his horny thumb, 'but the bastard's sharp enough to slit that fat cop's throat.'

But they were in for a disappointment. When the door was opened two hours later the pot-bellied guard had a companion at his side – a fierce, black-coated Alsatian

156

which bared its teeth and gave a vicious low snarl as soon as it saw them. The Yank flashed Crooke a quick glance.

Crooke shook his head and the Texan relaxed his grip on the primitive knife clutched beneath his jacket. Sullenly they allowed themselves to be taken out to the taps and then to the latrines.

An hour later, after they had finished their coffee, Stevens was escorted into the cell by the same guard, holding back the Alsatian, which seemed only to be waiting for the opportunity to launch itself at the Destroyers.

The little cockney was pale and peaked, with dark circles under his eyes. His arm was bound up in a large crêpe paper bandage. Sitting down on the floor heavily, as they crowded round him, he said: 'The poor buggers ain't even got proper bandages.'

'How's it going, old lad?' Peters enquired softly.

'Fair to middling. But I must give that old rozzer his due. He's done his best for me. He called in the local sawbones and everything. But sir,' he turned to Crooke who was staring down at him anxiously, 'them Jerries haven't got nothing. Do you know, the MO had to take the slug out without gas. He froze the shoulder – that's all.'

Stevens grinned painfully when he saw their look of concern. 'Must say though, he gave me a fair old shot of that there Jerry gin before he started in on me with the carving knife. Proper treat it was.'

'How's the wound now, Stevens?' Crooke asked.

'It only hurts when I larf, sir. Don't worry about me. It'll take more than a bullet through the shoulder to make old Stevens kick the bucket.'

The Destroyers chatted about Stevens' treatment. Then Thaelmann asked, 'What they gonna do with us?'

Stevens' grin vanished. 'The old sarge told me that the Gestapo is coming to collect us this afternoon.' He held up his good hand hastily. 'Now don't wet your knickers. So far we're in the clear. As far as the sarge knows, they're coming to take us to Moosberg prisoner-of-war camp – it's about twenty odd miles from Munich. Stalag VIIb, it's called, with about twenty-five thousand Allied POWs of all nationalities – Poles, Russians, British, even Yanks – the lot. According to the rozzer, they'll investigate the killing of the blonde bitch there.'

The Destroyers absorbed the information. 'We could try to make a breakout from there, sir.' Peters broke their silence. 'Might be easier from a regular POW camp, especially if they've got an escape committee like.'

'I don't know,' Stevens said doubtfully. 'From what the rozzer said, it's a tough place to get out of. The local yokels get a reward for every *kriegie* they turn in and there's a special squad of police and dogs trained to chase up escapers. Besides I think there's a better way of getting out of this sodding mess.' Stevens winked solemnly. 'Have a look up my sleeve,' he whispered.

'But watch yer don't cut yer fingers!'

The Yank felt inside the sling and pulled out a scalpel. 'The four-eyed doc never saw me half-inch that one. He'll have to cut his toenails with the bread knife tonight,' Stevens said. 'But that's not all. Stick yer hand in the lucky dip again and see what you can find.' Jones did as he was told and this time produced a hypodermic. 'Jesus,' he breathed, 'what did you do, Stevens, steal the medic's whole goddam surgery?'

'Not quite, but almost,' Stevens said cheekily.

'But what are we going to do with them, Stevens?' Crooke asked.

'Well, sir, this is the way I think we can work it...'

# SIX

The two Gestapo men looked like cari-
catures of all the German secret policemen
the Destroyers had ever seen. The one was
tall and exceedingly thin, with a deathly pale
face and a red dripping nose; the other was
fat with great overhanging jowls. Both were
dressed in dark green leather coats that
reached to their ankles, with felt hats pulled
down over their faces. Both, too, had
stumps of unlit cigars stuck to their bottom
lips.

Officiously they pushed by the fat sergeant
standing at the door, hands dug deep in
their pockets, as if they were gripping their
pistols.

'What's that yer got in yer pocket – a
revolver, or do you love me?' Stevens said
with a trace of his old cockiness.

The fat Gestapo man ignored him. 'Search 'em,' he snapped at the sergeant. 'Search 'em thoroughly!'

'But I've already done so, *Kommissar*,' the police sergeant protested, 'when they came in.'

'You heard me,' the fat one barked. 'Search 'em. You country yokels are too trusting. I know these Tommy prisoners-of-war – they're cunning swine. They can find and lose fellers like you.' The fat one talked about the Destroyers as if they weren't there, not even deigning to give them a glance of idle curiosity.

With a shrug the fat sergeant, an apologetic look in his eyes, ran his plump hand over their bodies, while the two Gestapo *Kommissars* watched.

The sergeant stopped when he came to Stevens. 'What about him?' he asked. 'The wounded one.'

'Heaven, arse and twine, man!' the thin one cursed. 'What do you think this is – a kindergarten?' He shoved by the sergeant.

'Get out of the way, let me have a look at the Tommy swine!'

With the unlit cigar stump stuck to his bottom lip and his mouth open slightly, as if he were having difficulty in breathing, the tall Gestapo man bent and began to run his hands expertly up the sides of Stevens' body. He stopped at the left jacket pocket. He patted it again. Carefully he inserted his thin fingers, as if he were expecting to find a mousetrap in the pocket and brought out the scalpel, a look of triumph dawning on his skinny face. 'Now what have we here?' he asked unnecessarily, making the most of the find.

The fat police sergeant flushed scarlet. 'It must be ... be the doctor's,' he stuttered in embarrassment.

'It must be the doctor's!' the thin man mimicked. He slapped Stevens across the face. 'Swine!' he cried, but without anger, as if the blow and the curse were part of a well-tried and successful ritual of intimidating prisoners.

Stevens staggered against the wall.

'You thin streak of piss!' the Yank snarled, and crouched, as if he were going to launch himself on the *Kommissar*. But the fat sergeant had already drawn his revolver and was pointing it at the Destroyers threateningly, as if he hoped by this means to make up for his blunder. Against the wall, Stevens sagged with his gaze fixed on the flags, hiding the look of success in his eyes. So far everything was working according to plan. They had found the scalpel, as they had planned the officials should, but they hadn't discovered the hypodermic concealed in his sling. As Stevens had said, 'Give the average cop a little something and he's happy. He thinks he's done his day's work and his pension's okay.'

'*Gut,*' the fat Gestapo man said, satisfied with the search. He turned to the sergeant. 'Put that cannon away, man! We're in charge now. Get them handcuffed, ready for the transport.' He looked at his big flashy wristwatch. 'The Munich train'll be leaving in thirty minutes. And there won't be another one till tonight.'

'If there is another one!' the other man said dolefully.

'Now, now, Willi,' the fat one chided. 'That's defeatism, you know. You can get yourself in trouble with the Gestapo for talking like that.'

Willi thought it was a huge joke. He flung his head back and roared with laughter. The Yank looked at him scornfully and nudging the Guardsman whispered: 'Boy, this is gonna be as easy as taking candy off'n a kid!'

The little station platform, hung with a huge sign announcing that 'The Wheels are Turning for Victory', was crowded. Everywhere soldiers, laden with weapons and kit, and civilians, carrying huge suitcases or bearing sacks which looked as if they might contain potatoes, were staring up the track expectantly, waiting for the train to Munich. A couple of them glanced at the Destroyers, chained to one another by long handcuffs.

Then an officious peak-capped Reichsbahn station master pushed his way through them to the departure board and their attention was directed at him. Deliberately he changed the signs on the departure board which hung from a kind of signal arm above the platform. A great groan went up from the crowd when he was finished. *'Scheisse,'* Willi cursed next to Stevens, *'eine halbe Stunde Verspaetung!'* Stevens winked at Crooke twice. It was the signal they had agreed upon. They could start putting their plan into operation. A couple of rifle-carrying 'chain dogs' marched slowly down the platform.

They gave the Destroyers a hard look and nodded to the Gestapo men; then strode on majestically. Stevens waited till they had gone. 'I want to take a leak, mate,' he said in English.

Willi, the thin one, looked down at him. *'Was?'*

'A leak, mate,' Stevens repeated. 'Don't you understand English?' He held out his free hand to his flies as best he could and made a hissing noise. 'Pee. Make water. Take a load off me kidneys.'

'*Ach, so, du willst pissen?*'

'*Ja, ja,*' Stevens parodied him, '*pissen,* mate.'

Willi turned to the fat official. 'What do you say, Kurt?'

The fat one nodded. 'Yes, come on, let's take them. Then we won't have any bother with them in the train. You know what it's like then – there's always some stupid old woman getting locked in or something.'

Like a line of obedient schoolchildren, the Destroyers marched behind their captors towards the sign '*Abort*' at the far end of the platform.

The underground white-tiled lavatories, with a line of contraceptive machines on one wall and the sign '*Pst, der Feind Hoert Mit!*' on the other, were deserted save for an old woman. She sat at a little table, on which there was a saucer for tips and rolls of lavatory paper, her feet in carpet slippers and her face buried in a newspaper. Absently she looked up when they came in and turned to her paper again, as if she saw handcuffed prisoners brought into her little underground kingdom every day of the week.

'*Also,*' the fat one barked at Stevens, '*los, pis man!*'

The little cockney looked at the grey-haired toilet attendant and shook his head. 'We don't do that sort of thing in England, mate,' he said. 'Not in front of ladies.'

The fat *Kommissar* looked at him blankly.

Stevens spoke loudly and deliberately, as if he were talking to an idiot, '*Nix pissen* in front of *Damen.*'

The fat Gestapo man stared at him incredulously. A slow grin started to spread across his broad face as he absorbed the information. 'Did you hear that, Willi?' He shook his head in mock disbelief. 'Funny lot these Tommies. I've always said so and I'll say it again.' He turned to the woman. 'All right,' he snapped, 'get yourself out of here for a minute.'

'What?'

'You heard, move.' He pulled out a metal

disc and stuck it under her nose. '*Geheime Staatspolizei*,' he rapped and grinned as she shot up and scurried away with surprising speed for such an old woman. He stuck the identity disc back in his trouser pocket. 'Now Englishman, will you do us the great honour of making water.'

Willi guffawed. He obviously thought it a great joke.

Stevens walked over to the urinal bowl, followed by the others, their eyes fixed anxiously on the door in case anyone else came in. The little cockney hesitated and went through the show they had rehearsed the night before. Holding up his bandaged hand in the sling, he said, 'And how am I supposed to get it out with no hands, eh?'

The Gestapo men might not have understood the words, but they understood the gesture. Willi grunted something and pulling out his keys, unlocked Stevens' handcuff.

The Destroyers acted at once. As one they pushed back the startled fat Gestapo official and grabbed hold of the door so that no one could open it from the outside. Before Willi could draw his pistol, Stevens had pulled the hypodermic from his sling and pressed its needle against Willi's arm.

At the door Thaelmann hissed in fluent German. 'Don't make a move – either of you! That syringe is filled with deadly poison!'

Willi's hand dropped away from his pistol at once. Behind, a fat flustered Kurt, pistol in his pudgy hand now, hesitated.

'Didn't you hear what I said?' Thaelmann rapped. 'Put that pistol down, or your friend will be dead within five seconds.'

The fat man looked from Thaelmann back to the deathly pale Willi.

Stevens helped him to make up his mind. He jabbed the needle a little harder against the leather of Willi's big coat. Willi gave a whimper of fear. 'Kurt,' he gasped, 'they mean it. *Kurt, do you hear me? They'll kill me if you...*'

He broke off suddenly as his comrade began to lower his pistol.

'*Hieruber mit der Pistole,*' Thaelmann

ordered. 'Throw it!'

Helplessly the fat one threw the pistol. The Yank caught it neatly and gave it a quick twirl round his finger like a movie cowboy. 'Gee, that feels good,' he cried enthusiastically.

Stevens nudged Willi. 'All right Wilhelm, you do the same nice and slow. To him.' He indicated Thaelmann.

Obediently Willi threw his pistol to Thaelmann who snapped: 'Now, the keys!'

The thin *Kommissar* did not hesitate. He threw them to Crooke. Seconds later, they were free and Thaelmann was pocketing the invaluable Gestapo identity discs.

Swiftly they gagged and bound the two Gestapo men with their own belts and braces and ripped up their shirts to make gags for them. Then they bundled them into separate cubicles. Gippo turned the discs of the cubicles to *Besetzt* – occupied – and banged them closed on the two Gestapo men, whose eyes bulged with frustrated rage above their gags. 'Have a nice long sit,' Stevens said airily, as they hurried out.

On the platform the crowd began to shuffle expectantly. The Munich train was coming in earlier than expected. Their eyes fixed on the track, the Destroyers nearly bumped into the fat, carpet-slippered toilet attendant. She looked at them in bewilderment. Obviously she was asking herself how they came to be free so suddenly. But Gippo was up to the situation. He took out a handful of coins he had stolen from her saucer. 'Here,' he said magnanimously, like some prosperous businessman distributing largesse, 'for you.' His German, learned by peddling dirty postcards to German tourists at Port Said before the war, was terrible but understandable. 'Our comrades are having a long sit – with paper, you understand?'

'*Mit Papier*,' she echoed. '*Jawohl, vielen Dank, mein Herr.*' Pleased with her tip, she shuffled back to her underground post.

Five minutes later the Destroyers were safely aboard the train and comfortably settled in a first class compartment with the aid of the Gestapo identity discs.

# SEVEN

It seemed that all the sheds, stables, barns and garages in Bavaria had opened their doors to spill their contents on to the country roads. The Destroyers, trudging steadily southwards to the Austrian border, had never seen such a chaotic mess of contrivances. There were brand new Opels and Horchs, mixed up with ancient open-sided farm carts drawn by plodding oxen or aged flea-bitten nags. Bicycles, dog carts, wheelbarrows even – anything that could move on wheels, all packed high with the refugees pathetic little domestic treasures.

The farmers sat glumly with their women on top of the piles, while the leather-breeched youths and the younger women marched along the roads, many of them barefoot, their precious shoes tied around their necks. Here and there, a boy beat a flock of squawking geese in front of him with a switch or dragged a reluctant goat behind.

No one paid any attention to the Destroyers; the column was full of foreign farm labourers who were fleeing with their former masters. On all sides they could hear French, Russian, Dutch and several other languages they could not identify. As Crooke had said when they joined the column southeast of Munich: 'Nobody's ever going to check this lot. There are far too many of them – and you can bet your life that some of those old farmers have forgotten to bring their identity documents with them.'

Twice he had been proved right. Once a column of *Tigers* had appeared, obviously heading to the front where Patton had broken through, bull-dozing everything in their path in their hurry. A little while later a high-ranking officer in a captured US jeep had stopped the column to bellow an apology, but he had not been the least interested in their papers. A few hours later

174

they had passed a hurriedly erected road-block, manned by elderly farmers with the armband of the *Volkssturm* – the German Home Guard – under the command of a couple of *Wehrmacht* NCOs in uniform. But the elderly conscripts, gripping their tall nineteenth century French rifles in skinny hands which hadn't held a weapon since the last war, had had no time for the refugees. Their anxious gaze was fixed on the west, as if they expected to see old 'Blood an' Guts' come roaring over the fields at the head of his tanks at any moment, firing at them personally with his ivory-handled revolvers.

In spite of his weariness, Crooke was enjoying the march. The weather was wonderful, cloudless sky and a dazzling sun. But it was a sun which brought little warmth, for there was a faint wind blowing all the time from the snow-capped mountains in the distance which marked the frontier. The temperature was just right for a long march – cool and bracing, with little dust in spite of the long line of slowly moving traffic.

But Thaelmann was not too happy with it. A couple of times he sniffed the air anxiously and frowned to himself. 'What's up with you?' Stevens said finally. In spite of his wound, he was keeping up well. 'You look like a wet weekend in Wigan.'

'It's going to snow,' Thaelmann announced in his dogmatic German fashion.

'Give over,' Stevens said scornfully. 'Snow in April!'

'It won't be the first time; they've had snow in Bavaria as late as June,' Thaelmann said sourly. 'Believe you me, we'll have snow before the day's out.'

'You know the area?' Crooke butted in.

'I was in Dachau for eight months before I escaped, sir. It's quite close to Munich, you know. When I got out, the local CP there hid me with the farmers down here till I could get over the border on my way to Italy and Africa.' He grinned at the memory: an unusual thing for him. 'They told the locals that I was a Catholic priest on the run. You see they're all one hundred per cent black – er Catholic – down here. They were only too eager to hide the *Herr Pfarrer.* Once a couple of them even asked me to read the mass. That was a close call, I can tell you.'

'Religion – the fish and chips of the working masses, mate,' Stevens quipped. 'That's what your old Charlie Marx said before they planted him in Highgate Cemetery.'

For once Thaelmann was not offended. 'In this particular case, religion was a pretty useful opium, I can tell you.'

The conversation lapsed again and they concentrated on the march to the mountains, as the road got steeper and the temperature began to drop.

About three o'clock that afternoon, the column began to pile up where the little side road entered the main highway to the south. The Destroyers threaded their way through the mess of carts and cars. A group of German MPs had set up a roadblock at the crossroads and were checking passes. They had come to a high-ranking officer in a big black Horch, who was protesting volubly at the delay. But the MPs were obviously not satisfied with his papers. Doggedly they turned the pages of the documents, stopping occasionally to make a whispered comment. The Destroyers pressed closer to the little scene at the crossroads. Then they saw the officer's face for the first time under the gleaming black peak of his cap. The Yank gasped: 'Will you get a load of that!'

'Stone the sodding crows,' the Cockney breathed. 'It's him – all dressed up like a Jerry officer!'

'Who?' Gippo asked, his view blocked by Peters' shoulders.

'Falk – the bastard who betrayed us – *Major sodding Falk!*'

From their vantage point, the Destroyers took in the little scene.

Falk's shabby jacket and overlarge jackboots were gone and now his breast was covered with German decorations and medals. Crooke identified the Iron Cross, the German Cross in Gold, the Silver Close Combat Badge; there were several other bits of cheap gilt and brass he couldn't identify. On his shoulders he wore the silver stars of a major.

But the hard-faced sergeant in charge of the German MPs was obviously not impressed by either the decorations or the Major's papers. With a brisk wave of his hand, which indicated he had made up his mind and wanted to get the column moving again, he ordered Falk to drive the car up to the farmhouse which the MPs were using as their command post. A couple of MPs sprang on the running board, machine pistols clenched in their hands. Slowly Falk drove off. Moments later he disappeared into the white-painted house. He had been arrested.

As the column started to move forward again, Stevens, crouched at the side of the road, turned to Crooke. 'Are you thinking the same as I am, sir?'

Crooke nodded, not taking his gaze from the house into which the OSS Major had vanished. The two MPs had posted themselves at the door like sentries. Obviously they thought they had made a catch. 'Yes, I think so, Stevens – we want Falk.'

The Yank gave a slow grin of anticipation. 'That I'm looking forward to, skipper.'

As they slipped away from the road to wait for the darkness, the first soft flakes of snow began to drift gently down.

# EIGHT

The wind blew steadily from the mountains. The night was icy. Around them the snow-white plain was bare and empty. All was silent.

Crooke looked at his watch and shivered uncontrollably. It was after midnight. Time to go. 'All right, lads,' he whispered, his breath fogging the air. 'Time to move out.'

Stiffly they rose from their hiding place and began to spread out cautiously as he had instructed, the crunch of their boots making what seemed a devil of a noise to Crooke. But the men in the house slept on, unaware that Death was approaching.

They reached the house. By the light of the stars Crooke could see the maize cobs from the previous autumn still drying under the wooden eaves. He waved his hand to left and right. As they had planned, the Yank and Peters, who were armed with the Gestapo pistols, stole round the other side of the house. Thaelmann and Gippo took their positions on Crooke's right. Stevens, who was of little use in this venture because of his wounded arm, crouched behind them. Crooke licked his lips. There was a soft click as Gippo released the blade of the flick knife he had taken from Willi.

'Remember,' Crooke whispered, not taking his gaze off the house, 'we want them out of there. Once they've barricaded themselves in, we're done for. We won't be able to get them out with our two pistols. After all they're armed with Schmeissers.' He nodded to the German. 'Okay, it's up to you now, Thaelmann.'

The German wet his lips. *'Bist du das, Hans?'* he whispered, as the others tensed.

Dead silence was the answer. The wind continued to blow softly.

Thaelmann tried again. He raised his voice a little this time. *'Hans, hoerst du mich nicht?'*

Inside there was a sleepy grunt as the sentry, who they knew was posted just behind the door, woke up. 'Mensch, *wer ist da?*' a grumpy voice answered.

Crooke put his finger to his lips to indicate that Thaelmann should not reply.

Heavy boots dragged themselves to the door. A rusty chain clattered. A bolt squeaked back. A second later, a tousled blond head, minus helmet, peered round the door. The sentry had a machine pistol in his hands. For a moment he was silhouetted, a stark black shape against the yellow light from within the farmhouse – a perfect target.

Gippo aimed and threw his knife. The sentry's hands flew to his chest. His machine pistol clattered to the ground. Before he could fall, Crooke and Thaelmann had rushed forward and supported him. Noiselessly they lowered him to the ground. Before he touched the snow, he was already dead.

Peters grabbed the machine pistol. They ran down a long corridor, heavy with the smell of winter hay and animals. Peters pointed to a light shining beneath the door of a room at the end of the passage. 'There.'

Crooke nodded. 'I see.'

Those who announced their presence in such operations as this with a pleasant 'good evening' didn't live to continue the exchange of niceties. He drew a deep breath. Then he flung the door open and jumped back hastily. Peters, his legs thrust wide apart, swung from left to right, spraying the room with his deadly fire. In the close confines of the little whitewashed *Stube* he could not miss. When he had finished the smoke parted to reveal two of the MPs dead on the bloody floor. The three remaining men – all wounded – were pressed against the walls in terror, holding up their blood-smeared hands.

Crooke pushed Peters aside. '*Wo ist der Offizier?*' he rapped.

'*Unter im Keller,*' the sergeant gasped, as he began to slump to the floor, trailing a bloody stain down the white wall behind.

At the information, an ugly grin of unholy anticipation started to spread over the face of the Yank. As Crooke turned to search for the cellar, the Yank poked his pistol through the door and pressed the trigger three times – quickly. There were no survivors.

Falk's welcoming smile fled almost as soon as it had come when he saw the grim looks on the faces of the men who crowded into the cellar. But he tried to brazen it out: 'Jesus, am I glad to see you guys. It's colder than a witch's tit down here! I thought my papers were the real McCoy. I would have sworn they would have gotten me through any checkpoint. But somebody back in the OSS workshop in Berne must have slipped...'

The babble of words ended in a gasp of pain as the Yank slapped him hard across the face.

'Hey, what the hell's the matter with you?' he cried. 'You gone nuts or something–'

The Yank hit him again. A thin trickle of blood came from his right nostril.

185

'Shut up!' Crooke hissed. 'And don't hit him again till I tell you to.'

'Wilco,' the Yank muttered. 'But don't make me wait too long.'

Crooke did not waste words. 'Why did you betray us to the Jerries?' he snapped. 'What's your game, Falk?'

'Come off it, Lieutenant,' he faltered. 'Me help the goddam Krauts! You must be kidding!'

'Hit him, Yank,' Crooke ordered tonelessly, without taking his gaze off Falk's face.

'With pleasure, skipper.'

He drew back his fist and smashed it into Falk's face with all his strength. Falk's head jerked back and struck the dirty wall. Blood spurted out of his nose.

Crooke gave him a moment while he fumbled in his pocket and produced an elegant white silk handkerchief. He held it to his face where it turned a deep red almost immediately. 'Now come on, Falk, we've not got all night to waste on you.' Crooke's voice rose in feigned anger. 'What's your game?

Why did you turn us over to the SS?'

'I didn't really,' he said thickly. 'It was Karel the Czech. He's the boss.'

'What do you mean the boss?' Stevens snapped. 'You're a major and he's only an other rank.'

'Yes, but he's the real boss of our cell.'

*'Cell?'* Crooke queried.

'Yes,' Falk lifted his eyes to the British officer's face. 'We are all members of the Communist Party.'

'But if you are a communist,' Thaelmann said, 'like I am, why betray us to the enemy?'

Thaelmann's declaration that he was also a communist must have seemed like a ray of hope to Falk. He took the blood-stained handkerchief from his nose. When he spoke his voice was firmer and more confident. 'It wasn't you,' he said, directing his attention at Thaelmann. 'Don't get me wrong. Not you fellers at all. Karel said you were just pawns in the game. It was your mission, you see! As soon as Colonel Petrov found out your mission, he radioed us to get rid of

187

you. I wanted to send you off on a wild-goose chase, but Karel was insistent. He said that...'

'Shut up!' Crooke interrupted. 'What did you say? Colonel Petrov ordered you to get rid of us?'

Falk nodded. 'We were working with him,' he said slowly, as if he were suddenly aware for the first time of exactly what he had done. 'You see the new Europe must be a communist Europe. The Russians have not fought this long war to see the old capitalist plutocrats take over in Central Europe...'

'Enough of that mumbo-jumbo,' Crooke said. Beside him the Destroyers stared down at their prisoner in utter disbelief. 'What the devil has all that got to do with our mission to kill the Hawk?'

Falk hesitated. 'Because,' he whispered, '*Obersturmbannführer* Habicht is one of us.'

# NINE

Gippo and Stevens handed round great doorsteps of black bread and *Wurst* and steaming mugs of coffee. Falk's eyes fixed on the coffee greedily and he licked his blood-caked lips; but no one offered him a mug.

For a while there was silence, broken only by the soft rustle of the wind in the snowy pines outside and the hungry champing sound the Destroyers made as they wolfed down the first food they had eaten that day. The Yank belched appreciatively. 'Boy, that chow sure tasted good!' he sighed. Stevens swallowed the last of his thick sandwich, which Gippo had carefully cut into small squares for him, as if he were an invalid and couldn't have digested it otherwise. 'Yer right there, mate,' he said. 'Even the fact that this wog here' – he indicated Gippo – 'made them with his dirty black fingers couldn't have put me off that grub.'

Gippo beamed, in no way offended.

Crooke wiped his mouth and turned back to Falk. 'All right, Falk,' he commanded, 'give us the story.'

But the break had seemed to reinforce the little man's will to resist. 'I'm not saying anything else,' he said through lips which were tightly pressed together. 'You can do what you like but you're not going to get me to talk!'

Crooke looked at the Yank.

'It's a helluva waste of good java,' he snarled. He drew his hand back and brought it forward swiftly, before anyone could stop him.

The full contents of the mug flew into Falk's face. The little OSS man screamed as the scalding hot coffee struck him. 'You bastards!' he cried, holding his face in both hands and rocking from side to side on the little stool. 'You've blinded me!'

'We haven't – *yet*,' Crooke said without pity. 'Now wipe your damn face and talk!'

Falk wiped his face hurriedly. 'I don't know all the details. All I know is what Petrov told me,' he said. 'But apparently in the summer of 1944 Habicht started to see which way the wind was blowing. Like most of the Krauts in his kind of position he began to look for a way out. But how? He had a bad record. The Western Allies wouldn't touch him. The Russians were different. They were more pragmatic. They were prepared to use anyone, even a member of the Reich's Main Security Office, if he could help to bring the war to an end more swiftly. At all events, Habicht used the Warsaw Rising last summer as a means of getting in touch with the Red Army on the other side of the Polish capital. Our people realized at once that he would be no earthly use to them in some POW camp. In return for the promise of his freedom and a new start after the war, Habicht agreed to go back to his unit and work for us. In the confused fighting in the

Warsaw sewerage system and the tunnels, a lot of Germans got cut off from their units. When they rejoined their outfits nobody questioned them about where they'd been. It was the same with Habicht. He returned and played his old role, as if he had never even heard the word Russian.' Falk paused for breath.

'So you mean to say,' Crooke said in a shocked low voice, 'that the Hawk is working for the Russians?'

'Yes.'

'Then what the devil is he doing running this Werewolf organization in the Alpine Redoubt?'

Falk hesitated.

Crooke nodded to the Yank. He drew back his clenched fist. Falk's hands flew to his face to protect it. 'Okay, okay,' he cried hastily. 'Well, the longer the Western Allies are held up by the Werewolf and the Alpine Redoubt, the better chance the Red Army has of establishing itself in Central Europe.'

'You mean grabbing more territory?' the

Yank said.

'No, no, not that at all. The Russians are a peace-loving people. They will allow the peoples there their freedom. That is why they are prepared to work with criminals like Habicht. Don't think it was easy for any of us…'

'Enough!' Crooke snapped, his mind full of what General Patton had said to Mallory and him in the staff car on the way back from Ohrdruf. He turned to his men. 'Do you understand now?' he asked. 'The Alpine Redoubt business is being used by the Russians as a means of holding up the Americans and deflecting us from our original aim of capturing Berlin and Prague. Montgomery's people in the north and the American 9th Army on the Elbe have been kicking their heels for two weeks now instead of pushing on towards Berlin because Eisenhower felt he would need all of his strength to overcome the Werewolf and the Redoubt. And behind it all is Stalin. The Russians are controlling the Werewolves through the Hawk.'

Thaelmann looked at him. 'But that can't be true, sir! The Russians are loyal allies! They want to see this war brought to an end as quickly as possible. Haven't they suffered more than any others? Twenty million dead! They wouldn't use a Nazi swine like that Habicht.' He swung round and grabbed Falk by the jacket. 'You're lying, you little bastard,' he yelled. 'The Russians would not do such things!'

Falk sighed. 'No, I'm not lying,' he said softly.

For a moment the two communists were frozen there, their faces almost touching, while the Destroyers stared at them in silence.

Falk broke the silence. 'Be a realist,' he said. 'Why so moral? When we no longer need Habicht, he can be gotten rid of. Men like him can be used and then disposed of like one would – a tool, some tool that is no longer required.'

*'Moral!'* Thaelmann exploded. 'It's nothing to do with morality, man. It's *my* life – and

the lives of a lot of little people in Germany like me! What do you know of what it was like to be here in Germany during the Depression before the Nazis took over? Six million unemployed and the Party the working class's only hope. That swine Hitler taking over and then for those who didn't rally to the Party living underground with every man's hand against you. Dachau with those swine in black beating you up and worse at the drop of a hat. And then twelve years on the run, living in other countries that didn't want you and got rid of you as soon as it was expedient.' Thaelmann's face burned with rage. 'And you – you,' he stuttered, 'you from your nice safe America, three thousand miles away from it all, ask me to compromise. To associate with a bastard like Habicht, who helped to kill my comrades...' The thought was too much for Thaelmann and he broke off, his chest heaving.

'Come on, mate,' Stevens said with surprising gentleness and feeling. 'Let's go upstairs. I'll fix yer another cup of coffee.'

'Yes, let's all go upstairs,' Crooke added. 'The stench in this place is unbearable.'

Slowly they filed up the stone steps, leaving Falk slumped on the little stool.

Just before dawn they completed their preparations. With their usual skill at 'finding things before they goddam get lost', as the Yank often cursed, Gippo and Stevens had organized enough food to last them for the next two days. The MPs' bodies had been hastily buried under the snow and the traces of the massacre removed. Now, armed with the weapons they had taken off the dead 'chain dogs', the Destroyers, muffled in what extra clothing they had been able to find in the house, were standing around ready to move off.

'What about Falk?' Peters asked the question they had all been waiting for someone to ask for the last hour or so.

'Yes, Falk,' Crooke said thoughtfully and looked at the Yank.

The Yank nodded and took out his pistol.

'Let me,' Thaelmann said softly. 'I think I

should. After all, this is the end of something for me.'

Silently the Yank handed him the pistol. Thaelmann took it and turned. Slowly he opened the door to the cellar. They heard his feet clatter down the stone steps.

For a moment there was no sound save the harsh expectant breathing of the men standing motionless in the passage. Suddenly a scream cut the night air. It was followed by one single shot.

When Thaelmann came up from the cellar, the pistol still in his hand, there were tears in his eyes. 'Come on,' he said, not looking at them. 'For God's sake, let's get the hell out of this place!'

They followed him outside, their boots crunching on the frozen snow. But none of them noticed the faded emblem he had dropped – a well-worn red star badge, with a cheap gilt hammer-and-sickle in its centre. Unknowingly, Gippo bringing up the rear, crushed his heel on to it. It disappeared into the snow.

## Section Three

## HELL VALLEY

'So the big bird has come to roost. I guess it's up to the Destroyers to wring that particular bird's neck, eh?'

*The Yank to the rest of the Destroyers,*
*18 April, 1945*

# ONE

Shortly after six on the morning of 18 April, 1945, the Destroyers reached the Hoellenthal and started climbing through the pines that grew up the base of the mountain.

There was no wind, but it was bitterly cold. Crooke, in the lead, plunged straight up the steep slope into the dense pine forest through the grey mist.

The snow got deeper. The pine forest was full of noise – the crunch of their boots and the rustle of branches above them, heavy under the weight of frozen snow. In spite of the looted extra clothing and the exertion of climbing, they soon started to feel the cold. The snow which had penetrated their clothing began to melt with the heat of their bodies. It soaked their clothing. Within half an hour they were wet and frozen to their waists.

But Crooke did not dare stop. He knew they must be high up the mountain before the sun came over the top and exposed them to any observer surveying the slope with his field glasses. He forced them to keep up the killing pace.

The two hours which followed were a nightmare of back-breaking exertion, complicated by the fresh snow which began to fall. They stumbled, fell and rose again on the slippery white surface, forcing their bodies to continue, peering through the streaming white mass with screwed-up eyes for some suitable cover.

By ten o'clock they were coming to the edge of the forest. Somewhere in the white swirling mist above them was the naked mountain top and Schloss Hoellenthal, but they could not see it.

Then, when the forest had almost run out, they came upon a cave. It was on the side of a ridge, where the wind had scooped out hollows like huge teethmarks. It was not much of a place, but for the frozen, exhausted Destroyers, it was more than enough. One by one they scrambled through the narrow entrance, away from that terrible, merciless white rain and slumped on the rocky floor in exhaustion.

The sun, blood red and joyfully warm, shone over the white waste as they crawled stiffly out of the cave and crouched in the rocks which surrounded its entrance. In silence they stared at the beautiful sweep of valley below and then up to the castle which brooded above them on the naked peak. 'Schloss Hoellenthal,' Crooke broke the silence.

'The castle of the valley of the dead,' Thaelmann translated.

They studied the place they had come so far to attack, taking in every aspect of the sinister structure.

It was not one of the medieval affairs that dot the valleys of the Rhine or Moselle. Schloss Hoellenthal was a nineteenth

century edifice with fake Gothic battle-
ments and towers, but with large French
windows which would have been the despair
of any robber baron concerned with
defending himself against attack.

Yet the expert gaze of the Destroyers
noted all the signs of a well-constructed
defensive position: the concertina wire
barriers on both sides of the one access
road; the little skull-and-crossbones signs
which indicated minefields; the machine-
gun pits; and everywhere soldiers in the
peaked cap and mountain boots of the elite
SS mountain troops. Habicht might be the
leader of the Werewolves in the Alpine
Redoubt, but he obviously did not trust his
safety to the rabble of Hitler Youth and
German Maidens who made up the bulk of
his organization. 'That looks a tough
sonovabitch to get into,' the Yank said.

'What we need is a Halifax bomber,'
Stevens said, nursing his aching arm. 'A big
old blockbuster on the place and that would
be it. That Hawk wouldn't fly again...'

'*Duck!*' Crooke roared.

As one man they flopped into the snow and lay perfectly still as a Fieseler Storch, which had glided in from behind them, zoomed in for a perfect landing on the emergency airstrip on the cleared patch in front of the castle.

Carefully Crooke raised his head. Obviously the pilot hadn't seen them. He turned off his engine, then sprang down on to the snow. Officiously he opened the cabin door behind him to let his passengers get out. Crooke focused the field glasses he had taken off the dead MP sergeant and, holding one hand over them so that they would not sparkle in the sunlight and betray their position, he surveyed the two men who had emerged from the little spotter plane. The one he recognized immediately. He was fat and badly shaven, and in spite of the field-grey of the German Army, which he was now wearing, there was no mistaking him – it was the OSS radio operator Karel!'

The other man was tall and slim and for a

moment he kept his back to Crooke but as he turned Crooke caught the gleam of the SS runes on his tunic. However, it was not the runes nor the man's badges of rank, which indicated a senior officer, that held his attention. It was the great beak which dominated his face. *Obersturmbannführer* Habicht was as ugly in real life as he had appeared in the snapshot which Mallory had shown him back in London.

'What is it, sir?' Peters asked anxiously.

'The Hawk has arrived,' Crooke announced. 'He's just got out of the Storch with Karel.'

The Yank whistled softly through his teeth. 'So the bird has come to roost. I guess it's up to the Destroyers to wring that particular bird's neck, eh?'

Crooke smiled: 'I guess you're right, Yank.'

# TWO

They spent most of that afternoon surveying the castle, around which there was a great deal of activity. Half-tracks and Volkswagen jeeps kept coming and going, labouring their way up the steep approach road. At regular intervals, too, small groups of black clad Werewolves ventured into the deep snow to lay explosive charges and detonate them under the watchful gaze of one of the SS Mountain Division instructors; and once six boys staged an ambush among the pines. The Destroyers had a ringside seat as the panting youngsters fired their *panzerfausts* at a target propped up in the snow, but the projectile missed every time. The instructor jeered at them unmercifully and in the end broke off the exercise. As a punishment he made the boys crawl over the snow on their

207

stomachs pushing their rifles in front of them until they were soaked to the skin. Then he forced them to stumble back to the castle through the deep snow at a cracking pace.

Peters shook his head as they disappeared from sight. 'It's the same the whole bloody world over, ain't it?' he said to no one in particular.

Towards four o'clock, as the sun started to go down behind the mountain, it began to snow again and they retreated to the back of the cave to discuss the situation.

'As I see it,' Crooke began, 'there are two possibilities of getting into the damned place, either by the access road...'

'Which is too well guarded,' the Yank broke in, 'for us to have a chance in hell of bringing it off.'

Crooke nodded his agreement. 'Or by breaking into the ground floor. Those french windows look promising. If we could evade the guards, which shouldn't be too difficult in this kind of weather, then we might have a good chance...'

He stopped suddenly as a faint noise reached their ears. It was the baying of dogs.

'Well, that's put the mockers on that one, hasn't it, sir?' Stevens said. 'They've got our sodding four-legged friends out there too.'

He moved to the rucksack to break out the evening rations. They relapsed into a gloomy silence, while Stevens divided the black bread, onions and stale cheese they had taken from the farmhouse as best he could with his left hand and passed round each man's share.

'What we need is info,' Stevens said conversationally. 'Perhaps there's another way into the sodding place that we don't know about. I read a book once, and it said "knowledge is power". What we need is power. At the moment we're not punching clever. We need a prisoner.'

Crooke nodded in agreement, finishing the last of his cheese and onion sandwich. 'You're right, of course, Stevens. Without information we're fighting in the dark. But the question is how're we going to get a prisoner without stirring up the whole hornet's nest on the top of that hill?'

'Ambush on the road, sir,' Gippo suggested.

'That's not much cop. You can bet your life, Gippo, that that spotter plane watches it all the time.'

'The road is too risky,' said Crooke. 'We don't want to have to fight those SS chaps, if we can help it. What we want is some lone soldier. But I don't think we'll find anyone going out for a stroll in this weather, what do you think?'

'What about the kids?' the Yank suggested.

'You mean the Werewolves?'

'Yeah. You saw they were coming out to train all afternoon. Nobody would take any notice of any firing coming from their direction. Hell, they've been banging away all afternoon.'

'But wouldn't the others notice if they didn't come back?'

'You know how it is in the Kate Karney,

sir,' Stevens said. 'The average squaddie's a bit thick. Not much in the upper storey.' He swept his good arm round the Destroyer's frozen faces. 'I mean – look at this lot here. Not exactly the type of bloke you'd find in the Brains Trust, giving Professor Joad the old mental one-two. By the time they've tumbled to the fact that their mockers is not in the canteen or the craphouse, we'll either be in Brown's garden or up there in that stately home, sipping china tea with his nibs.'

The wind was rising steadily as the little group of Werewolves plodded into sight, heavily laden with explosives and bazookas. It was a bitter, icy wind which whipped up the snow in little white gusts round their boots and stung their frozen faces and forced them to lower their heads. All of them, that is, save the burly SS instructor of the day before who marched, face turned unyieldingly to the snow, a Spandau machine gun set on his broad, square shoulders as if it was a toy.

Silently the Destroyers, crouched in the thick pines, counted them as they came closer. 'Six of them,' Peters whispered, tensing his grip on the machine pistol. Crooke's gaze swept the little file of Germans and came to rest on the SS man, whose tunic was heavy with decorations – obviously an experienced soldier. The rest were little more than children.

'Poor little buggers,' Peters said, a look of genuine concern on his face. 'There's something wrong with the world when titches like that have to play soldiers. They should be at home with their mums, larking around with bats and balls.'

'Yeah, and you're talking a lot of balls,' the Yank sneered. 'Them little bastards would plug you just like that. Ain't I right, Thaelmann?'

Thaelmann mumbled something, but did not take his eyes off the little group of black-uniformed Werewolves.

Crooke knew Peters was right. But the

Yank was too. If the opportunity arose, those same children would kill without compunction. Perverted by their years of training in the Nazi creed, human life would mean little to them if it were extinguished in the name of the Greater Germanic.

'You take the instructor,' he whispered to Peters, 'as soon as they get into the cover of the pines out of sight of the castle.'

'And the kids?'

'Thaelmann will ask them to surrender. If they do, okay. If they don't.' He shrugged.

'But we need a prisoner, sir.'

'Of course. As soon as they've had a taste of lead, they'll begin to surrender, believe you me. We've got them in a perfect trap here. They'll have no alternative but to surrender.' But for once he was to be proved wrong.

In silence they watched as the little file slipped into the pines, hidden now from the castle. 'They've come far enough,' Crooke said.

Peters raised his pistol and steadied it on a

rock. He took careful aim. On both sides, the others did the same.

'Let them have it – *now!*'

The SS man spun round at the cry. The heavy pistol cracked sharply. The SS man threw up his hands in agony. The Schmeisser slipped from his shoulder and tumbled to the snow. He pitched forward after it without a sound. The Destroyers hesitated. Out of the corner of his eye, Crooke could see the revulsion on Peters' face, and he knew what the big man was thinking – must they kill the kids?

The children reacted first and Crooke ducked as a wild burst of fire splattered the rocks above them and whined up the gorge in a vicious ricochet. Next moment the Destroyers opened fire.

What followed was a massacre. The hail of fire from the rocks bowled them over like marionettes in the hands of some mad puppeteer. The whole business was over within half an minute, and six pathetic little bodies lay in a bloody heap below them. The

Destroyers, momentarily paralysed by this grotesque act of butchery, gazed at the scene in stunned silence. Then, suddenly, one of the bodies began to move, tried to get up. In an instant Peters was on his feet, plunging down the slope towards the wounded boy.

# THREE

Gently they carried the boy into the cave and laid him down. Crooke watched numbly as the hardened killers smoothed back his hair and wiped his forehead. He stared down at the boy's bloodless lips and trembling eyelids that showed he was alive.

'Is there anything you can do for him?' he asked. Peters looked up silently, his big hands covered with blood. He shook his head.

'He's had it,' Stevens said softly.

Slowly the boy's eyes flickered open, closed, flickered open again and remained thus. *'Wasser,'* he whispered softly. *'Bitte.'*

There was no urgency, no pain, no pleading in his voice. It was almost as if he had made peace with life, in the knowledge that death would be coming for him soon.

Gippo took their one canteen cup, scooped

up a handful of snow and pressed it between his hands, forcing out a few drops of liquid. He gave it to the boy, while Peters held up his head.

Crooke looked at the others. He knew what they were thinking. He had been wrong; the fanatical youths had fought and died where they stood. Already the snow was beginning to cover their dead bodies. As for their prisoner, he was dying visibly by the second. Yet they must have the vital information.

He made up his mind. 'Peters,' he snapped.

'Sir.'

'Take Gippo with you and check the bodies for food and ammo,' he ordered.

'But the lad, sir.'

'You heard me! Don't worry, we'll look after him the best we can.'

'You sure, sir?'

'*Of course I'm bloody well sure!*' Crooke exploded. 'What the devil do you think I'm going to do? Get on with it, man.'

Reluctantly Peters pulled up his collar and

nodded to Gippo. In silence they went out, bending their heads against the snow.

Crooke waited till the crunch of their boots on the snow had died away, then turned to Thaelmann. 'You know what we want from him?'

Thaelmann looked at him, shocked. 'But he's dying, sir.'

'A lot of lads like him have died already in this damned war and a lot more will die if we don't put an end to it soon.' Crooke felt his temples begin to throb violently. It was a sign that the splinters from the explosive bullet which had scooped out his eye in 1942 were at work again. Pain stabbed through an eyeball that was no longer there.

Thaelmann bent over the boy and propped him in his cradled arm. He forced a smile and whispered, 'It's all right, son. The pain'll go soon. But you've got to help us, if we help you.'

'How ... please,' the boy gasped.

'We want some information – about the castle.' He nodded hastily to Stevens. 'Get

219

him some water from the snow – quick.'

The boy looked at him curiously. 'English?' he asked.

'Yes, we're English soldiers.'

The news did not seem to worry him. 'I've never seen an Englishman before,' he whispered weakly. 'So … you are English.'

Thaelmann looked at Crooke as if for instructions. The boy had minutes to live. He had seen that look of death often enough in the Desert. 'We want a way into the castle – a safe way,' he said. 'Ask him that, Thaelmann. And quick! He's dying on us!'

Stevens let the boy have a few drops of water and then cleaned the sweat from his brow with a rag. 'All right, Thaelmann. He's all yours.'

Thaelmann put his questions and translated as the answers came from the boy's pale lips in faint, painful fits and starts. 'The *Obersturmbannführer's* office is in the tower … on the second floor… His private quarters are above it…'

'The guards?' Thaelmann asked, bending

his head now to catch the answers, which were growing ever fainter.

'Twenty of them ... from the SS... We have an honour guard though at his door.' In spite of the pain, a faint flicker of pride welled up inside the dying boy and was reflected momentarily on his face.

'Is the access road the only way in?' Thaelmann queried swiftly. 'No back entrance?'

The boy shook his head weakly. His strength was almost gone now. 'No other way...'

Crooke had a sudden idea. 'How do you boys get out if you want to get down to the village without the guards at the gate knowing you've gone? Try that one, Thaelmann.'

Thaelmann did as he was ordered.

For a moment, the dying boy did not speak. Then he smiled pathetically. 'Out ... oh, yes we got out... The sewers,' he coughed thickly and blood trickled from his mouth. Stevens wiped it away with the rag.

His lips formed the word *'danke'* and he

gave a feeble smile.

'Sewers,' Crooke spat out the word. 'Where do they come out? Ask him where they come out.'

Thaelmann translated Crooke's question and bent his head close to the boy's chest to catch the faint whispered answer. 'The tower – this side of the tower ... under the holly bushes ... a hole, right in the middle...'

Then the boy's head dropped to one side.

'He's dead,' Thaelmann said numbly.

Stevens bent down and slowly closed the boy's eyes with awkward hesitant fingers. 'Poor little nipper,' he whispered.

# FOUR

Soft-footed they padded through the thick curtain of falling snow. A faint yellow light at the iron gate of the Schloss illuminated the sentries, heads dug deep in their big rough collars, rifles slung over their shoulders. Behind them the black mass of the castle disappeared high into the night.

Carefully Crooke parted the branches of the bush. 'You first, Yank,' he whispered. The Texan did not need urging. He hurried forward, his head and shoulders thick with snow and disappeared into the bushes.

'Now you, Stevens.'

One by one they vanished into the bushes. 'All right, spread out,' Crooke whispered, 'and see if you can find the entrance to his sewer.' They knew whom he referred to, but the knowledge seemingly no longer had any effect. The boy had died twelve hours ago now; he had joined the many other innocents who had died in this war.

Gippo was the first to spot something. He picked up a piece of paper and held it up to his nose. 'Chocolate,' he said. 'Where there's candy, there's kids.' He bent down again and picked up an empty bottle of *Himbeersirop*. Then Stevens picked up a handful of fragments that made up a torn letter. 'Like a ruddy paper chase, ain't it,' Stevens said, when suddenly the snow broke beneath him and he disappeared up to his waist.

'What's up?' Peters whispered.

'What do you think's up, you silly sod,' Stevens answered. 'I've fallen into the bleeding sewer! There's a pong coming up here like a gorilla's armpit!'

All of them could now smell the stench which floated up from the hole. But they had no time to concern themselves about that. They had found the entrance to the sewer and it was high time they got out of sight of the sentries.

Moments later they were all crouched inside the evil-smelling tunnel, its low curved ceiling dripping with a foul, green liquid that fell into the thick, turgid scum at their feet. With a curse Crooke dropped his match, as it burned down to his fingers. The Yank lit another one and by its flickering light they advanced a few yards into the sewer until Crooke thought it safe enough to light the pine torch which Peters brought just for this purpose.

'Christ,' Stevens breathed, 'I feel like the bleeding Count of Monte Cristo.'

Gippo's dark eyes bulged with the fear of the unknown. 'It is very scaring in here,' he said, his teeth chattering.

'Come on, yer silly nig-nog,' Stevens said. 'Give us a kiss and I'll hold yer hand!'

With Crooke in the lead, they set off, crouched low to avoid striking their heads on the slimy ceiling, their bodies tense, weapons at the ready.

The sewer seemed to go on for ever, but Crooke knew that as long as it inclined upwards, they were on the right track. Obviously that was the direction it would follow to the interior of the castle.

Crooke glanced at the green blur of his wristwatch. They had been in the sewer ten minutes and there was still no sign of an exit. He began to get worried, but he said nothing. Another five minutes went by. Suddenly, to his horror, he noticed that the sewer was running downwards. Obviously it was leading away from the castle now. He stopped them.

'What's the problem, sir?'

'Firstly, we've overshot the mark. We're leaving the centre of the castle again. And secondly, how the hell do you get out of a sewer?'

'Simple, sir,' Stevens answered promptly. 'You have a manhole cover. When I was a kid in the Smoke, we used to nick 'em and flog 'em to the scrap iron blokes.'

'Of course, Stevens,' Crooke said. 'All right, turn about and let's see if we can spot a manhole cover.'

Five minutes later they found it, its position indicated by a steady drip-drip of melting snow into the centre of the green scum on the floor. Peters handed the Yank his torch and reaching up, placed his hands, palms outwards, on the slimy metal cover. He pushed. Nothing happened. He tried again. This time the cover gave. Carefully he raised it above the level of the snow. A faint pale gleam of light descended to them. Gently Peters dropped it on to the snow.

'You first, Gippo,' Crooke whispered, 'you're the lightest. But watch it!' Peters bent and Gippo sprang on his back, grasped the edges of the hole and in one and the same movement levered himself through. They thrust up his machine pistol and he took up his position just out of their sight, while they hauled themselves up and out, one after the other, sprawling in the snow, weapons immediately at the ready.

They were in the courtyard of the castle, surrounded on three sides by tall grey walls, their windows carefully blacked-out by thick curtains or shutters, from which came the muted sound of voices. Crooke cast a careful glance around the walls. 'All right, Gippo, put the cover back.'

They began to size up the place. From behind one of the windows came the crackle of loudspeakers. They tensed again and stared in the direction of the sound. Someone turned the radio up and they could hear the bombastic blare of the trumpets, followed by the strains of a Liszt prelude. They were cut off suddenly, as an announcer's solemn and sonorous voice began: *'Das Oberkommando der Wehrmacht gibt bekannt. In tagelangen schweren Kampfen gegen den massiven Angriff der US dritten Armee ist es unseren Truppen nicht gelungen...'*

'The news – it's the news,' Thaelmann whispered. 'Patton's Third Army has broken through.'

'Good. That'll keep 'em busy,' Crooke replied.

'In both ways, sir,' Thaelmann said. 'They've got to listen to the news. It's orders. That'll keep them out of our way.'

'Good. Okay, let's go.' They glided across the empty courtyard to the nearest wall. Like shadows they tiptoed to the corner. Crooke held up his hand. Cautiously he peered round it; then ducked back hurriedly. 'A sentry,' he whispered to Stevens who was behind him.

Crooke dropped to the snow and making the smallest possible target, craned his head round the corner once more. The man was coming in their direction, rifle slung over his shoulder. He could not fail to see them. He came closer and closer, his heavy boots crunching on the frozen snow. He was level with them now. Crooke tensed for a moment of discovery and the first crack of shots, which would alarm the castle and put an end to their whole mission.

The crunching footsteps continued past them and retreated. A moment later the sentry mounted the steps opposite them. A yellow knife of light slid into the night. A door squeaked open and was closed again.

The light disappeared. The sentry was gone.

'Thought they had us by the short and curlies then, sir,' Stevens whispered.

'I did too. Come on, let's get out of this damned courtyard. I feel as if I'm on the stage in some West End Theatre!'

Swiftly, like grey ghosts, they slipped round the corner and disappeared from sight.

# FIVE

Slowly the fat Czech, Karel, replaced the heavy blackout curtain and switched on the light again. For a moment he looked at his gross, unshaven face in the mirror in thoughtful contemplation.

It had been sheer chance that he had glanced out of the window when he did to check the weather, preparatory to making his own escape from Hoellenthal. But there had been no mistaking that tense lean face with its black eye patch, illuminated for a fraction of a second by the yellow light that escaped from the open door. And those dark shadows crouched – he knew who they were!

Karel picked up his codebook and dropped it again. He would not be needing it any more. Operation Redoubt was over. No doubt if and when Moscow sent him on another mission, the Director would provide him with a new code. The organization was very careful about their codes; it was a security measure that paid dividends. He knew he should really destroy the old book. But was it worth going through the fuss and bother of burning it and flushing the charred leaves down the latrine? 'The Red Air Force,' he said, talking to himself as most lonely men do, 'will take care of that for you soon enough.'

He continued with his packing, stuffing his rucksack with the thick wad of OSS dollars that he had taken from Gottwald's dead body. Originally Petrov had radioed him that he could use them to pay Habicht, but that had been before Patton's offensive had started and their man at SHAEF Headquarters at Rheims had come through with the definite information that Eisenhower had called off the attack on Berlin and directed Patton to lead the full strength of the US Army in a major offensive to capture the Redoubt. Now they no longer needed Habicht; the Redoubt had served its purpose well. 'And my dear *Obersturmbann-führer* Habicht,' he said aloud, an unpleasant grin on his greasy face, 'where you're going, you won't be needing any dollars.' He patted the thick wad of green notes. Moscow did not have to know about them. They would be his own private reserve, just in case.

Suddenly he realized what an idiot he had been. If those English fools started trouble, they would probably alarm the whole castle and hinder his departure – and to judge by the brief glimpse he had caught of their faces, they were going to do exactly that. Poking his head out into the corridor, he called softly: 'Kurt!'

Habicht's personal pilot, Hauptmann Kurt Held, came in, his handsome young face tense at the note of alarm in Karel's voice.

'What is it?' he said urgently. 'Habicht hasn't found...'

Karel held up his hand. 'Don't panic,' he said. 'Habicht has not found out what you're up to.'

'I'm not panicking, Karel, but you know Habicht. He's absolutely ruthless. He would not hesitate one moment, if he found out what you're...'

'*We*,' Karel corrected him. He had taken the measure of the ex-fighter pilot who had been assigned to Habicht after his Focke Wulf squadron had been wiped out over Schweinfurt the previous winter by the US 8th Air Force. He was another like Habicht, out to save his skin now that the tide had turned against Germany. 'But something else has happened which might affect our plan. How long will it take you to get the plane ready for take-off?'

'Thirty minutes. The cold start might take five to ten minutes. But I've got to light the flare path. Even the Fieseler needs a couple of hundred yards, especially at night, to get off the ground safely.'

'Good, drop everything else.'

'But my gear!'

Karel grinned. 'Where you're going, my friend, you will no longer be needing your fancy blue uniform. Those days are over.' His grin disappeared. 'Now down to the field with you. Don't let anything or anybody stop you. You can expect me soon.' He looked at his watch. 'But it's imperative we be off the ground and away from this place within thirty minutes. Do you understand – *imperative!*'

The young pilot shrugged his shoulders. 'If you say so. But I can't swear that the plane will start just like that.'

'If it doesn't, my friend,' Karel told himself, 'then you and I will be flying by means of our own wings.'

He waited till the pilot's footsteps faded away down the corridor, then he picked up the 'phone and dialled the extension.

The person he had called answered immediately, as if his hand had been tensed over his 'phone all the time. He listened attentively while Karel spoke.

'Thank you, Karel. I shall make a note of your information. *Ende,*' the voice said. Then the receiver went dead and the fat man was left staring down at it. Slowly he replaced it on the cradle, and talking to himself once more in the mirror, said: 'It is a pity about you, Habicht – a great pity. We could use you in the years to come.' He nodded to himself, as if confirming his own statement. Then he went back to his packing.

It was twenty minutes past nine. The Stormoviks would have already taken off from their field outside Vienna. By now they would probably have gained the necessary height and closed up in squadron formation. Soon they would be skirting the capital and heading south-west for Hoellenthal. There were exactly twenty-five minutes to go.

*'Mensch habe ich ein Husten!'* Thaelmann said hoarsely, his head bent so that the peaked-cap sentry in front of the entrance could not see his eyes. 'It's this damn climate up here. I

swear it's giving me pneumonia!'

The SS man swung round. *'Was machen Sie hier?'* he cried in alarm. *'Sie sind doch Zivilist.'* Hurriedly he fumbled with the strap of his machine pistol, peering at Thaelmann in alarm in the weak, yellow light. But he never freed the weapon. Gippo, who had sneaked up from the other side of the *Kommandantur* building, hooked a thin arm round his neck, pulled him backwards and, in the same instant, slid his knife into the man's ribs. The German's face contorted with pain. He opened his mouth to scream. Gippo threw up his elbow and blocked his cry. The knife thrust home once more. Blood burst out of the sentry's nostrils. Then he was dead.

Gippo lowered him to the snow and shook his head wonderingly, almost sadly, at the foolishness of the soldier for allowing himself to be taken so easily. Opposite him Thaelmann whistled softly. The rest of the Destroyers hurried round the corner. While the Yank and Peters stood guard at the door of the headquarters building, they threw handfuls of snow over the sentry to conceal him from view.

'All right,' Crooke said softly. 'That's good enough. Come on! You bring up the rear, Stevens!'

Swiftly they stole inside the poorly lit headquarters. As Stevens closed the door behind them, Crooke glanced at the brown board facing the entrance. 'There,' he said, *'Obersturmbannführer* Habicht – second floor.'

As softly as they could they ran up the steps, keeping to the edge of the stairs where they didn't creak. Before them lay a gloomy corridor.

There was no mistaking *Obersturmbannführer* Habicht's office. A great black hawk was painted on the door, its ugly yellow talons clutching the symbol of the dying regime a blood-red swastika. Crooke wasn't an imaginative man, but the thing seemed to sum up the essential vulgarity of the One Thousand Year Reich, which had lasted exactly twelve.

He hesitated at the door. Stevens grinned. He read Crooke's thoughts at that moment exactly. 'Funny, ain't it, sir,' he whispered, 'we've come so far to do this and now we don't know what to do exactly. Do we knock or what?'

Crooke had a flash of total recall: Colonel Keyes, Campbell and Sergeant Terry rushing into Rommel's HQ in their attempt to assassinate the 'Desert Fox'; Geoffrey Keyes crying 'well done' just as the German grenade landed in the hall; and dying on the grass verge outside the house a moment before the blast of German machine-gun fire had ripped out his own eye.

What a long way he had come since then! Mission after mission; and now they were almost at the culmination of their last one. He couldn't afford to let it fail. His Destroyers must survive the hostilities.

'All right, lads,' he said softly, and before he could stop himself, he repeated the old old cliché of a man going into action. *'This is it!'* Taking a deep breath he grasped the door handle, pressing it down hard and marched into the room, the Destroyers behind him.

The Hawk was as ugly as the agent's snapshot had shown him to be. He looked up almost casually, in no way surprised, it seemed, by the ragged men who had suddenly burst into his dark-panelled office with a great green-tiled stove in the corner. He sat there behind the desk, neat, dapper and almost debonair in his black uniform. The Hawk was patiently calm, collected, correct and utterly evil.

For what seemed an age no one spoke. Then the Hawk licked his lips. 'So you are the celebrated Destroyers,' he said in excellent English. 'Karel has told me about you.' He looked around their faces slowly with a certain clinical interest, like a scientist taking a last look at his animal specimens before dissecting them in the laboratory.

'You're a damn confident bastard,' Crooke said, made uneasy by the man's calm.

'Why not, Crooke? That is your name,

isn't it? I recognize you. The eye, you know.'
He touched his huge nose gingerly, almost
as if he were reassuring himself that it was
still there. 'We have our defects, don't we?
But you know, Mr Crooke, it has always
been my theory that the perfect, handsome
athlete never gets anywhere in this world.
You see, he has everything, beauty, strength,
and attraction for the female sex. Why
should he exert himself? It is the chap with
one leg shorter than the other, the crippled
hand, the disfigured face who has to work at
life, achieve something, be...'

'Shut up!' Crooke snapped. 'We haven't
come here to listen to a discourse on the
meaning of life!'

'Why not?' Habicht said easily. 'After all,
life is only important when we discuss it.
But I am quite happy to change the subject.
Don't you think you've backed the wrong
side?'

'What the hell do you mean?'

'Well, my dear fellow, we Europeans have
to start selecting sides now, haven't we? After

all, your economy is ruined, your people weary, your Empire in ruins. You need a powerful friend. Do you think the land of boundless possibilities, as we call the United States in German, should be that ally?'

'And do you think that you have achieved anything by your change of loyalties?' Crooke retorted. 'All you have done is to swap one evil system for another. I suppose you wanted to be on the winning side, come what may, eh?'

The blow hit home.

The Hawk's face flushed. 'You and your decadent English lords,' he snarled. 'Do you think there is any hope for you even if you win this war? You belong to a tired, divided nation that has lost both its money and its spirit. What can you become – save a lackey of the Amis?' He rammed home his point. 'Great Britain and the British Empire are finished!'

'What the hell do you know about it?' Crooke shouted at him. 'All you're concerned with is saving your precious hide.

Yank, get rid of the bastard for me. I've had enough of him.'

'With pleasure, skipper.'

The grinning American raised his machine pistol and pointed it at the Hawk's heart.

But before he had pressed the trigger, a voice snapped: *'Haende hoch!... Na wirds bald?'*

# SIX

'*Keine Bewegung,*' the same menacing voice ordered. 'You move and you die!'

An SS lieutenant holding a machine pistol emerged from behind the big green-tiled stove. Other soldiers pushed aside the curtains and moved into the room. All were heavily armed and all were pointing their weapons at the Destroyers.

The Hawk leaned back in his chair and stroked his monstrous beak of a nose with deliberate slowness, as if he wished to show his captives that he was savouring his moment of triumph.

'How did you know?' Crooke asked.

'A little bird told me,' the Hawk answered with a cold smile, 'five minutes before you entered my office so abruptly.' He turned to the lieutenant and said in German: 'Take a look at them, *Sturm*. The English select their killers well, don't they? A Red, a nigger, an Ami and the scum of the English slums.'

'And you,' Thaelmann said in the same language. 'What about you, a hired traitor, ready now to abandon the sinking ship like a dirty...'

Thaelmann reeled back clutching his bleeding mouth, as one of the SS soldiers hit him squarely across the face with the muzzle of his pistol.

Out of the corner of his eye, Crooke saw the SS lieutenant flash a strange glance at Thaelmann, then back again to the Hawk. But his gaze was concentrated on the Werewolf commander. He knew what must be going through the man's head: the Destroyers would have to be got rid of – at once! With their knowledge of his double dealing with the Russians, they presented a grave danger to his own security.

The Hawk reached into the drawer of his desk and brought out a small, snub-nosed automatic. He checked to see that the magazine was firmly in place, ramming it home with the butt of his palm.

Crooke glanced at his men. Their faces were pale and strained, but there was no fear in them. They were prepared to accept their fate stoically, as if they had known all along from the very day he had brought them out of the baking-hot Egyptian prison that this was the way it would have to end.

The Hawk clicked off the release. He raised the little pistol. The young SS men backed out of the way. The Hawk's eyes had not changed; they remained dark, cold and utterly empty. He would kill them without any feeling whatsoever.

Suddenly there came the thick cough of a plane motor from outside, muffled a little by the snow and the thick curtains of the office. The Hawk lowered his pistol a little, a look of annoyance on his face. 'What the devil was that?' he asked.

The lieutenant hurried over to the curtains. He pulled them aside slightly and peered out into the falling snow. For a moment he did not speak. The plane motor coughed again and died after a few stutters. 'It's your Storch, *Obersturmbannführer*,' the young officer reported, swinging round and revealing the surprise on his face.

'What!'

*'Jawohl!'*

'But that's impossible!' He rose and looked out into the darkness. *'The swine,'* he snapped, as he recognized Karel, his precious rucksack slung over his shoulder, yelling at the pilot swinging the propeller. 'They're running out on me...'

His words were drowned by the scream of the first Stormovik dive-bomber, come to eradicate the evidence of the Red Army's short-lived co-operation with the German Werewolf Organization. Outlined by the light of the flares being dropped by its comrades, it fell out of the sky in a screaming power-dive, plummeting straight for the castle.

The Hawk stared at it horrified, as dozens of bombs came wobbling down all around the castle. They exploded with a soft hiss, spurting burning white phosphorus everywhere. A sheet of white flame sprang up and at once it was as light as day.

As the first dive-bomber pulled away and zoomed back to the rest of the squadron, the next came roaring down. At four hundred miles an hour it hurtled at the circle of white flame.

Then the first of the high explosive bombs erupted in a thick blast of smoke and a bright orange sheet of flame. At the window the Hawk reeled back screaming, his hands clutching his face.

'*Obersturmbannführer*,' the lieutenant cried, his voice hysterical with fear. He caught hold of the wounded Hawk and pulled away his blood-stained hands. Where the grotesque nose had been there was a great hole.

The lieutenant screamed and drew his blood-smeared hands away, as if he had been stung suddenly. 'My God,' he quavered. 'What have they done to you?'

Meaningless sounds came from the Hawk's

lips, as he staggered towards the Destroyers, his hands outstretched like a blind man feeling his way.

Then another Stormovik was on them. The Destroyers flung themselves to the floor. Beneath them, the wooden blocks rose like a rough sea. The great blast of super-heated air swept into the room. It seemed an age before the explosion came.

A gigantic invisible hand plucked up the Hawk and smashed him against the great green stove. The tiles gave and as the red-hot shrapnel whizzed through the room bowling over the SS men, he lay there, dead. 'Come on,' Crooke shouted above the stammering of the German machine guns and the howl of another Stormovik. He staggered up to his feet, pushing aside the dead SS man who had slumped over him.

A young blond soldier without a helmet tried to get in his way. Crooke kneed him savagely. The lieutenant fumbled for his machine pistol in the rubble. The Yank kicked him in the side of his helmeted head.

He reeled back.

Crooke staggered to the door. 'Follow me,' he yelled.

The Destroyers scrambled after him. They pounded down the corridor, the sound of their boots drowned by the roar overhead. A skinny boy in leather pants emerged from a room, a Hitler Youth dagger held in his small hand. 'Stop,' he cried in determined falsetto.

The Yank stopped in his tracks and raised the pistol he had taken off one of the dead SS men. Peters blundered into him deliberately. 'No more killing,' he yelled. 'We've had enough.'

He brought his fist down on the boy's hand. The knife clattered to the floor.

Outside in the courtyard there was complete confusion. Bare-headed officers were running round blowing whistles. Sergeants were pelting back and forth yelling orders which nobody obeyed. Up on the crumbling walls, a youthful Werewolf crew still operated the anti-aircraft machine gun. Another bomb exploded and, when the smoke had cleared, the gun and its operators were gone.

The Destroyers skirted the barrack block and doubled past a burning truck. 'Where are we going, sir?' Gippo gasped.

'The sewer.'

Another bomb came whining down. They ducked automatically as it struck the wall behind them. The wall shook violently. From high above them great blocks of grey stone started to fall into the cobbled yard. In the flash of the exploding bomb, someone spotted them crouching over the manhole cover. Tracer stitched the air. The next moment Crooke yelped and bit back the pain in his shoulder. 'The Jerries never could shoot straight,' he gasped.

'Attaboy skipper,' the Yank cried enthusiastically. 'I'll show the bastards!'

He stood up, feet wide apart, and, ignoring the burst of tracer, he fired carefully at the men huddled around the Spandau. The gun went silent.

As a white pillar of flame streaked into the

night, tearing the heart out of Schloss Hoellenthal, Peters prised the manhole cover open and they were scrambling through and dropping into the foul liquid below. The castle's ammunition magazine had been hit.

As they raced down the sewer, explosion after explosion racked the castle. Hot waves of acrid air struck them in the face. But nothing could stop them now. A final thunderclap of an explosion flung them momentarily to the ground, but in an instant they had scrambled to their feet again, the burning hot blast whipping their ragged clothes around them as they ran on. And then they were thrashing their way through the bushes into the open.

To their right, on the emergency landing strip, the small spotter plane they had seen the day before was already burning fiercely. In its skeleton cabin the two men it was designed to carry eastwards were already shrivelled, mummified black pigmies. Behind them towered the evil outline of the ruined castle, tongues of flame leaping up its walls.

Stevens slipped off his sling so that he could run better. 'Come on, you jammy buggers,' he cried. 'Yer've seen the big picture. This is where we came in. Let's get the sodding hell out of here!'

Laughing like a bunch of boys just released from school, they plunged into the snow. Moments later they had disappeared into the trees.

# SEVEN

Cautiously the six-wheeled US Staghound armoured car edged its way round the corner. Standing next to the unshaven scruffy US lieutenant in his stained green ODs on the turret, an elegant officer in the dark-blue uniform of the Royal Navy stared curiously up the cobbled road. Two hundred yards away the first of the apartment houses which marked the start of the suburbs rose up against the darkening sky.

For a minute the lieutenant surveyed the houses through his binoculars; then he spoke into the throat mike. Somewhere inside the radio began to crackle, as the gunner operator confirmed to the 'can', covering them two hundred yards to the rear, that the armoured car was going to move into the suburb.

'Okay, roll 'em,' the lieutenant ordered.

The Royal Navy officer clutched the nearest stanchion, his other hand poised over his .38. The 18th Cavalry, to which the Staghound belonged, had already lost two armoured cars that morning. But the Boche were about finished. Their resistance was just token stuff, the last-ditch efforts of callow youths eager for a hero's death, and grizzled professionals who didn't know how to stop fighting. Now everyone knew that the Alpine Redoubt had been a myth, the Boches' last great propaganda victory, which had completely fooled the Allies – for a time.

The lieutenant spoke into the throat mike. 'Joe, take her the first left and the third right up to the intersection. According to my map, the Kraut precinct station is there.'

Next to him, the Navy man shook his head in mock bewilderment. The Americans seemed to have each town taped down to the last detail; yet they had been taken in one hundred per cent by the Redoubt business.

With a squeal of brakes, the Staghound

pulled up outside the police station which was guarded by two fat and very frightened *Schupos,* trying to ward off the excited crowd of jabbering foreigners.

When they saw the olive-drab armoured car with its bright white star, they forgot the policemen. They swarmed round it at once. Some of them had faces so pale and thin that the Commander wondered if there was any blood in them at all. A couple of them walked on crude crutches, empty trouser legs flapping as they hobbled after the others. Immediately the two officers were swamped by cries in half a dozen languages. The driver came up top and started to throw down K rations and cigarettes. Tears streamed down the former prisoners' faces as they grabbed them.

With difficulty they forced their way through the crowd.

'*Der Kommandant?*' the Naval officer snapped.

'*Jawohl, Herr Admiral,*' the policeman cried.

A few moments later he was showing the police major photographs of the six men he had been looking for these last five days.

'Do you know them?' he asked coldly, knowing in advance what the major's reply would be: the same apologetic negative he had received in every newly captured German town.

The major looked at the blurred snapshots carefully. Like the good policeman he was, he was not going to be stampeded into a hasty judgement, even by this strange British admiral, who spoke such excellent German. Finally he said: 'Oh yes, I know them. Ever since the colonel took over the town the day before yesterday. Good man, the colonel...'

The officer's face lit up. 'You really mean – you know them?'

'*Natuerlich*,' the major beamed, pleased that his information seemed so important to such a high-ranking officer as the admiral. 'Everybody here does. They're at *Rathaus* now with the staff. The colonel has collected a large administrative staff.'

'Come on,' the admiral called enthusiastically, cutting off the rest of his sentence. 'Let's go!'

'*Aber wo, Herr Admiral?*'

'*Zum Rathaus natuerlich.*'

'The colonel's staff,' the major announced as they entered without knocking. An attractive dark-haired girl with big breasts and a group of bemedalled junior officers rose to their feet hastily when they saw the Allied uniform. 'To see the Englishmen,' the major announced.

The girl clicked a switch on the office intercom and said something in rapid German. 'One moment, please. They will see you almost immediately.'

The naval officer opened his mouth to protest but, before he could do so, a white-coated orderly appeared with a trayful of glasses. Behind him another orderly carried a tray on which were several bottles of cognac. The major poured drinks all round and the bewildered British officer found himself in the midst of a social hour with the German officers.

The intercom crackled. The girl clicked down the switch. 'The Mercedes,' she whispered to one of the officers. 'They want the Mercedes outside in five minutes.' She looked up at the naval man. 'You may go in now, Admiral.'

The British officer remembered he was a gentleman and bit back the words which had sprung to his lips. Hastily the police major sprang to his feet. He opened the door. *'Der Herr englische Admiral,'* he announced.

'Tell him to get his skates on and get in here,' a well-remembered cockney voice said cheekily.

In a luxuriously-furnished office six men in elegantly tailored new uniforms sat in deep, upholstered chairs and stared at him solemnly, trying to fight back their laughter.

*'Well, I'll be damned!'* he cried.

Stevens put down his big cigar. 'Commander Mallory of Naval Intelligence, I presume?' he said calmly. With a brisk nod, he indicated that the blonde in the low-cut blouse with dark circles under her eyes, who had apparently been taking notes, should go.

'Administration, you know,' he explained, waving his cigar airily. 'Been swamped in it, ever since we took over. Housing, babies, rations – people wanting to know what to do with their daughters.' He winked at the girl. 'Not much of a secretary, that Gerda, but she has her points,' he said.

'But the uniforms,' Mallory protested, 'and all this?' He looked at Crooke for explanation.

Crooke merely looked across at the little cockney, sitting behind the big desk so confidently, as if he had been running towns with populations of twenty thousand or so all his life.

'Had to be dressed right, Commander. After all the First British Control Unit has to keep up face. The Germans respect that kind of thing, you know.'

'*The what?*' Mallory exploded.

'First British Control Unit.' Stevens pointed to the hastily painted sign on his desk.

Mallory peered at it, then read out the gold letters slowly. *'Colonel R Stevens, D.S.O – O.I.C. First British Control Unit –*You?' he breathed in open-mouthed awe.

*'Us.'*Stevens answered and began to laugh.

The great man was still in bed when Major Desmond Morton ushered Mallory and the Destroyers in. The counterpane in front of him was strewn with the typed foolscap sheets of his victory speech which he had been working on all day.

He yawned, showing that he had taken his false teeth out. With his bare gums and smooth round cherubic face, he looked like a great, cigar-smoking baby.

He saw their eyes fall on to the sheets of paper and grinned. 'In a few hours' time I go to the House of Commons and inform those members present that the war with Germany is over. An hour or so later I go on the wireless and tell the people of these islands that the war with Germany is over. At three o'clock this afternoon, in company with the legislators of this realm, I go to St Margaret's, Westminster, and tell Almighty God that the war with Germany is over.' He took a puff of his cigar. 'I must be prepared, you see.'

Then his grin vanished and his face assumed that of his bulldog look, the one the Destroyers knew well enough from the wartime newsreels: a mixture of spoiled child and angry animal. 'So the Russians were behind this Alpine rubbish after all?' he snapped, having a little difficulty with his 's's.

'Yes, sir,' Mallory compromised with his old principle that only God and the Monarch should be addressed as 'sir'. 'Naval Intelligence has definite proof of that.'

Churchill peered at the elegant Commander over the top of his glasses.

'That is good for Naval Intelligence, Commander Mallory. Let me tell you that when I took over the Admiralty in 1939, the DNI did not even know where the German fleet was.' He sighed suddenly. 'But that was a devil of a long time ago, a long time ago.' He repeated the phrase as if it signified something private to him. 'We have come a fair way since then,' he continued. 'But we still have to make sure that in Central Europe the simple and honourable purpose for which we entered the war is not brushed aside or overlooked in the moment of our success. It is the victors who must search their hearts and be worthy by their nobility of the immense forces that they wield.' He paused while the Destroyers stared down at him in bewilderment.

Churchill broke the silence again. 'But I wanted to see you again before you break up – this is the intention, Commander Mallory, isn't it?'

'Yes, sir. Today the Destroyers will be broken up as a unit.'

Churchill's eyes twinkled mischievously. 'That is a shame,' he commented. 'In the months to come, I could make use of rogues like you. You have cocked a snoot at the Hun for long enough. I have a feeling that we might have to deal with another nation of infinitely more cunning soon. Menzies could use men like you.' He referred to the head of MI6. 'The peace will be a hard one, you know.'

Stevens broke the silence. Looking down at the Prime Minister, he said firmly, 'No thank you, sir. We think we've done our bit. It's time we got back into civvy life. Me and the lads here have had a bellyful.'

Churchill looked at his smart cockney face. 'A bellyful, eh,' he echoed, rolling the word round his toothless mouth. 'That's what people are thinking, are they?'

'I don't know what the rest are thinking, sir,' Stevens answered hastily. 'I only know what me and the lads think.'

Churchill gave them a couple of minutes more, asking desultory questions about the Redoubt. Then he lost interest in that way of his. He started to glance at the sheets spread

out over his bed. Morton nodded signific-
antly. The great man did not even look up as
they shuffled out in silence.

After the rain of the early morning, the sun
was shining on the dense crowds which now
packed the centre of London. Many of them
sported multi-coloured rosettes, some comic
paper hats. Union Jacks were everywhere.

A group of women pushed a wheelbarrow
past them. A Guards officer sat on it, blowing a trumpet, followed by an American
sailor trying to get some sound out of an
old-fashioned gramophone horn.

Peters looked at the laughing, drunken
crowd which followed the wheelbarrow and
shook his head. 'An officer from the Brigade
playing a trumpet,' he sighed. 'I never
thought I'd live to see that!'

'It's peacetime, you big dope,' Stevens
chortled. 'Liberty Hall. Kiss me quick, yer
mother's drunk!'

A buxom woman in an apron made of
Union Jacks, performing a drunken tango

with a bespectacled clerk to the tune of 'South of the Border,' stopped them outside a tube station. To Crooke it seemed as opportune a time as any to get away. He took one last look at their faces. They had fought with him in Africa and all over Europe. But that was already the past. The British Empire was in danger; there were new battles to be fought. He touched his khaki beret with the winged dagger of the Special Air Service set in its centre in a kind of salute. 'All right, lads. Thank you for all you've done.'

He turned and began to make his way through the crowd at the entrance to the tube.

His departure seemed to take the heart out of the other Destroyers. They chatted together for a while and a couple of times Gippo whistled at drunken servicewomen. But Mallory noticed that Thaelmann kept looking at his watch furtively, as if he were impatient to get to Croydon and the 'plane which was waiting there to take him back to

Germany. The Yank was bored with the whole thing too. His sour yellow killer's face revealed all too clearly the boundless contempt he felt for the civilians milling all around them. Even the good-humoured, normally patient Peters kept looking down at his hands curiously, as if he were already trying to visualize them laying bricks after a lifetime of wielding a deadly weapon. Only Gippo and Stevens, the two inseparable rogues of the Destroyers, seemed to be enjoying the atmosphere of VE Day. Perhaps they already saw in the civilian foolishness an ideal opportunity for the fat pickings of the future.

Before they drifted away, Commander Mallory took a last look at them. For a while they had been projected out of the shallow materialism of their previous lives. They had touched the heights. Now the great days were over. They were returning to the dreary cynicism of the petty materialistic life to come.

'I suppose,' he said to no one in particular,

'that that just about ties up the Destroyers'
history, eh?'

'I suppose it does, sir,' Peters said, the last
to go. He touched his cap. 'The best of luck,
sir.'

'And you,' said Mallory. 'Goodbye, Peters.'

The publishers hope that this book has given you enjoyable reading. Large Print Books are especially designed to be as easy to see and hold as possible. If you wish a complete list of our books please ask at your local library or write directly to:

**Magna Large Print Books**
Magna House, Long Preston,
Skipton, North Yorkshire.
BD23 4ND